"Mommy, whe...

Justine's little son asked. "Who is that man? He's got a baby, too!"

Justine cast a glance at Roy. He was staring at her and Charlie. She couldn't tell exactly what he was thinking, but it was quite clear that the appearance of her son wasn't pleasing to him. And suddenly she knew she'd been right all those years ago....

"Yes, honey. Mommy found the babies and the sheriff has come to help find out where they belong. Now will you go get Aunt Kitty? The sheriff would like to speak with her."

Charlie raced out of the room. Once the boy was out of sight, Roy released a long breath he hadn't realized he'd been holding.

"You have a son?" There was an odd look of betrayal on his face. As though he knew...but no. No one, not even her sisters knew that Roy Pardee was Charlie's father....

Dear Reader,

This April, let Silhouette Romance shower you with treats. We've got must-read miniseries, bestselling authors and tons of happy endings!

The nonstop excitement begins with Marie Ferrarella's contribution to BUNDLES OF JOY. A single dad finds himself falling for his live-in nanny—who's got a baby of her own. So when a cry interrupts a midnight kiss, the question sure to be asked is *Your Baby or Mine?*

TWINS ON THE DOORSTEP, a miniseries about babies who bring love to the most unsuspecting couples, begins with *The Sheriff's Son*. Beloved author Stella Bagwell weaves a magical tale of secrets and second chances.

Also set to march down the aisle this month is the second member of THE SINGLE DADDY CLUB. Donna Clayton, winner of the prestigious Holt Medallion, brings you the story of a desperate daddy and the pampered debutante who becomes a *Nanny in the Nick of Time.*

SURPRISE BRIDES, a series about unexpected weddings, continues with Laura Anthony's *Look-Alike Bride*. This classic amnesia plot line has a new twist: Everyone believes a plain Jane is really a Hollywood starlet— including the actress's ex-fiancé!

Rounding out the month is the heartwarming *A Wife for Doctor Sam* by Phyllis Halldorson, the story of a small town doctor who's vowed never to fall in love again. And Sally Carleen's *Porcupine Ranch,* about a housekeeper who knows nothing about keeping house, but knows exactly how to keep her sexy boss happy!

Enjoy!

Melissa Senate
Senior Editor
Silhouette Romance

Please address questions and book requests to:
Silhouette Reader Service
U.S.: 3010 Walden Ave., P.O. Box 1325, Buffalo, NY 14269
Canadian: P.O. Box 609, Fort Erie, Ont. L2A 5X3

THE SHERIFF'S SON

Stella Bagwell

Silhouette
R O M A N C E™
Published by Silhouette Books
America's Publisher of Contemporary Romance

To Thelma and Gerald
with love and appreciation

SILHOUETTE BOOKS

ISBN 0-373-19218-5

THE SHERIFF'S SON

Printed in U.S.A.

Books by Stella Bagwell

Silhouette Romance

Golden Glory #469
Moonlight Bandit #485
A Mist on the Mountain #510
Madeleine's Song #543
The Outsider #560
The New Kid in Town #587
Cactus Rose #621
Hillbilly Heart #634
Teach Me #657
The White Night #674
No Horsing Around #699
That Southern Touch #723
Gentle as a Lamb #748
A Practical Man #789
Precious Pretender #812
Done to Perfection #836
Rodeo Rider #878
*Their First Thanksgiving #903
*The Best Christmas Ever #909
*New Year's Baby #915
Hero in Disguise #954
Corporate Cowgirl #991
Daniel's Daddy #1020
A Cowboy for Christmas #1052
Daddy Lessons #1085
Wanted: Wife #1140
†The Sheriff's Son #1218

Silhouette Special Edition

Found: One Runaway Bride #1049

*Heartland Holidays Trilogy
†Twins on the Doorstep

STELLA BAGWELL

lives in the rural mountains of southeastern Oklahoma, where she enjoys the wildlife and hikes in the woods with her husband. She has a son, a wonderful daughter-in-law and a great passion for writing romances—a job she hopes to keep for a long time to come. Many of Stella's books have been transcribed to audiotapes for the Oklahoma Library for the Blind. She hopes her blind audience, and all her readers, will continue to enjoy her stories.

BIRTH CERTIFICATE

Baby Boy: *Adam?*

Eyes: Green

Hair: Barely there!

Age: About two months

Mother: ~~UNKNOWN~~

Father: ~~UNKNOWN~~

Baby Girl: *Anna?*

Eyes: Green

Hair: Adorable red curls

Age: About two months

Mother: ~~UNKNOWN~~

Father: ~~UNKNOWN~~

Chapter One

Justine Murdock flexed her aching shoulders and shook her long red hair in the wind blowing through the open pickup. It was June in New Mexico. The sun was warm, and the orchards and pastures had just been washed with an overnight rain.

As the pickup rattled over a planked bridge crossing the Hondo River, Justine breathed in the fresh evening air. It was wonderful to be out of the medical clinic. She'd had an especially tiring day, and all she could think about was getting home to the ranch, taking a long, hot bath, then setting down to supper with her family.

The Bar M Ranch spread over several hundred acres at the foothills of the Capitan mountains. The house itself was built in a square, with a small courtyard in the center. The pink stucco walls, red tiled roof and ground-level porch, with arched supports, made the home a typical hacienda-style ranch house.

A graveled driveway circled the house, but since her sisters parked their vehicles in the back, Justine always used the front entrance.

Leaving her mud-splattered pickup in the shade of a pi-ñon pine, Justine walked the short distance to the porch, rubbing the back of her neck as she went. For some unexplainable reason, half the mothers of Lincoln County had decided to bring their babies in for their immunizations today. Each time Justine jabbed a fat little thigh or hip, horrified shrieks had echoed through the whole clinic.

Rubbing her furrowed brow, Justine glanced around her. It still seemed like she was hearing babies crying!

She saw it then. The straw laundry basket on the flat concrete porch, the tottery little head wavering just above the rim.

Running the last few steps to the porch, Justine knelt beside the basket. A loud gasp rushed past her lips. There wasn't just one baby sitting on the fuzzy blue blanket, there were two! A girl in pink, with bright red hair, and a boy in blue, with slightly darker auburn hair. Their features were almost identical, right down to the green of their eyes.

Dear God, twins! Where had they come from?

Quickly she scanned the area back over her shoulder. There were no strange vehicles parked nearby, no one to be seen. Did her sisters or aunt not know the babies were out here?

She looked back down at the twins, her face still mirroring the shock of finding them. "Where did you two come from?"

Distracted by Justine's voice, the babies suddenly stopped their fussing and stared, wide-eyed, at her. After a moment, the boy stuck out his lower lip and the girl began waving her arms in the air.

"Yeah, I know," Justine said. "You can't talk yet. You're not old enough."

Quickly she picked up the basket of babies and carried it into the house. "Aunt Kitty! Rose! Chloe! Is anyone home?"

No one answered as Justine carried the heavy load into

the kitchen and placed it carefully on the long Formica table.

With one hand still on the basket, Justine glanced at the refrigerator door, where notes were usually left, beneath an array of colorful magnets. A tiny square of paper dangled beneath a banana.

Charlie and I have gone to the grocery store in Ruidoso. Be back before dark. Love, Aunt Kitty

Justine groaned. It was nearly two hours before dark. That meant it would probably be at least an hour before her son and aunt returned home. As for her sisters, she doubted either of them would show up any sooner. Since their father's death six weeks ago, which had left them in dire financial straits, both Rose and Chloe had taken to doing the work of the wranglers they'd been forced to let go.

"Well," Justine said to the twins. "Looks like it's just you and me, kids. What are we gonna do?"

Now that the two had an audience, the twins didn't seem too perturbed at being confined to a laundry basket. Thankful for small favors, Justine thrust her hands through her thick red hair and tried to calm her racing mind.

Of course, she'd heard of babies being left on doorsteps in books or movies. But that was fiction. That didn't happen in Hondo, New Mexico. And certainly not to Justine Murdock.

What should she do now? What did a person do when she found deserted babies on her porch? she wondered wildly. And they were obviously deserted. No one was knocking at the door or calling on the telephone to claim them.

A thought suddenly struck her, and she quickly made a search around and under the babies for a note, or any sort of clue. The only things she found were two bottles and two pacifiers, wrapped in several disposable diapers. The bottles were filled, and the formula was still cool, as though the bottles had only been taken out of the refrigerator a short time ago.

Her nursing instincts kicking in, Justine picked up the boy, gave him a quick inspection, then did the same with the girl.

They were both plump, the boy a little more so than the girl. Their skin was clear and pink, their eyes were bright. Both babies appeared to be perfectly normal and healthy.

Satisfied with her examinations, Justine set the twins facing each other in the basket, then stepped back and studied them thoughtfully. From what she could remember from her own son, and from the babies she saw in the medical clinic, she would guess the twins to be somewhere around five months old. Neither one had any teeth, yet they could both sit up without any props.

Try as she might, Justine couldn't remember any of their friends or neighbors in the area having twins in the past six months. Nor could she remember twins of this age visiting the clinic at any time. Did that mean they weren't from around here? If so, why would anyone bring them to the Bar M?

Maybe her aunt or sisters would have some idea, but Justine doubted it. She figured the three women were going to be just as flabbergasted to find the twins here as she'd been.

You know you're going to have to call the sheriff, a voice said inside her head. Whoever had left the babies had committed a crime. Technically, the law needed to be advised and an investigation started. But calling the sheriff was the last thing on earth that Justine wanted to do.

Her legs suddenly wobbly, Justine pulled out a chair from the table and sat down. The babies stared at her, gooed and banged their little fists against the sides of the basket.

Justine smiled at their sweet round faces, while inside

her stomach churned sickly. More than five years had passed since she saw or talked to Roy Pardee, the sheriff of Lincoln County. And during the year and a half that she'd been back home in Hondo, she'd carefully avoided any contact with the man. He was a part of her past that she wanted to keep in the past.

But now she had two strange babies on her hands, and he needed to know about them before the trail from where they came from turned cold. Dear God, could she face him again? Could she look at him and pretend that nothing had ever happened between them?

The questions made her hands tremble, but when she looked at the two helpless children, her jaw set with determination. She wasn't an innocent twenty-year-old anymore. She was a mother, a nurse, a strong, grown woman. Someone had dumped two precious humans, and they deserved her help. Roy Pardee be damned!

Before she could lose her courage, Justine went over to the wall phone, located at the end of a row of cabinets, and punched the number listed for the Lincoln County sheriff.

A female dispatcher answered on the first ring, and Justine quickly gave the woman her name and address and went on to explain the problem.

"If you'll hold a moment, Ms. Murdock, I'll see how quickly someone can get out there," she told Justine, then went off the line. Seconds later, she returned. "Sheriff Pardee will be right there, Ms. Murdock."

In spite of all her earlier bravado, Justine felt as if the wind had been knocked from her. "Oh, it isn't necessary to send him. Any deputy will do."

The dispatcher must have considered Justine's suggestion strange. She paused for long seconds, then said, "In a case like this, Sheriff Pardee would rather see things firsthand."

"Oh, yes, of course," Justine said, glad the woman

couldn't see her red face. "Then I'll be here waiting for him."

The woman thanked her, then hung up. Justine placed the receiver back on its cradle, then groaned loudly. "I'll be waiting for him," she repeated with a snort, then turned and looked at the twins. "What am I saying? I won't be waiting for him. I'll simply be here—ready to talk to…whoever shows up. But I won't wait on Roy Pardee. Not even for you," she added to the babies.

As soon as the words were out, the girl began to cry. Justine quickly went over and lifted the baby into her arms.

"It's all right, honey girl," she said in a soothing voice. "Not all men are like Roy Pardee. Besides, when you grow up, you'll be a lot smarter than I was. You've got an intelligent little face. I can already tell you'll know to steer clear of men who walk with a swagger and wear a badge in place of a heart."

The trip from Carrizozo, where the sheriff's department was located, to the Bar M was a bit over forty miles. She figured she had thirty minutes or more before Roy arrived. She used part of the time to make a quilt pallet on the living room floor for the babies.

While the twins rolled and stretched on their new bed, Justine peered out the windows, toward the corrals and barns, in hopes of catching a glimpse of Chloe or Rose. If there had ever been a time she needed the support of her sisters, it was now. But there was no sight of them anywhere, and she could hardly leave the babies alone to go in search of them.

As for her son and aunt, Justine hoped the two of them didn't show up until after the sheriff had come and gone. She didn't want Charlie to see Roy. And she didn't want Roy to see her son. Maybe that was selfish and ridiculous on her part. Roy would probably never make any sort of connection. Still, she wasn't ready to take that chance. She wasn't sure she'd ever be.

Grimacing, Justine sat down on the couch in front of the twins' makeshift bed. More than likely, she thought, Roy had forgotten all about the brief affair they had nearly six years ago. Yet she hadn't forgotten. She couldn't. Charlie was a constant reminder of the time she'd spent with Roy.

As she watched the twins examine each other's ears and eyes, a soft smile curved Justine's lips. Having Charlie far outweighed the heartache and humiliation Roy had dealt her all those years ago. Her son gave her life meaning and purpose. She loved him fiercely, and would do anything to protect him. And knowing that only made her wonder how any mother had been able to leave these two babies behind.

It had been at least two years since Roy was on the Bar M Ranch. He'd stopped by on a trip to Picacho to see Tom. There'd been a rash of cattle thefts at the time, and he'd wanted to see if the ranch had suffered any losses.

Roy had always liked the older Murdock man, and had been sorry to hear of his sudden death a few weeks ago. Yet he'd not gone to the funeral. He'd known that *she* would be there and he'd decided that if or when he ever saw her again, he didn't want it to be over her father's grave.

That day, he'd chosen not to see Justine. But today he had no choice, and he didn't know how he would feel to finally look at her beautiful face once again. And she would still be beautiful. She could only be twenty-five or twenty-six now.

He didn't know exactly when Justine had returned home to Hondo. Quite by accident, he'd overheard someone in a Ruidoso café talking about Tom having his middle daughter back out on the ranch again. That had been several months ago, yet he could still remember how the snippet of news had stunned him. He'd come close to casually questioning the person about Justine's coming home. But he'd stopped himself short of doing such a thing. When the county sheriff asked questions about anyone, it always started the gos-sip mill grinding.

Six years ago, he'd been a young deputy in the middle of a messy breakup with the sheriff's daughter when Justine came into his life. The result had been a secret affair. To this day, he didn't think anyone knew about the torrid li-aison he'd had with the fiery-haired Murdock girl. Except him. And it annoyed the hell out of him, because he couldn't forget.

The knock on the door startled Justine, making her hands jerk as she fastened the adhesive tab on the waist of the diaper.

"He's not going anywhere." Justine spoke in a hurried hush to the boy twin. "And I want to make sure your pants aren't going to fall off."

Her heart beating in her throat, Justine took another mo-ment to check the fresh diaper she'd placed on the baby. Then, rising to her feet, she went to answer Roy's second knock.

The thin strips of glass running the length of the oak door gave her a glimpse of a tall man dressed in blue jeans, boots and a khaki shirt. His head was turned toward the corrals and barns, but the moment Justine opened the door, it jerked around to face her.

For long seconds, Justine could only stare at him and wonder why, after all these years, he should still look so good, so sexy, to her. The years she'd been away had changed him very little, except to add a few sunlines to his face and muscular weight to his body.

"Hello, Roy."

Beneath the brim of his black Stetson, his blue eyes flicked impassively over her face. "Hello, Justine."

She didn't realize just how much seeing him had affected her until she stepped back to allow him entry into the house. Her legs were trembling on weak knees, and for a moment she clung to the doorknob for support.

"Please come in. The babies are right here."

He stepped past her. Justine shut the door and turned to him.

"Were you the only one here when you found the babies?" he asked.

No "How are you, it's good to see you, how have things been?" Justine thought. He was going to be strictly business. That was good, she supposed. She didn't want anything personal to pass between them. Still, his indifference hurt. She'd once given him so very much of herself. But she supposed Roy Pardee was like so many men in this world. They took a woman's heart, then forgot all about it.

"It appears that way. My sisters must be out on another part of the ranch. And my—aunt has gone into Ruidoso."

He was looking at the two babies now. Justine drew in a shaky breath and raked her fingers through her long, tangled hair.

"What time was it when you came home and found them?"

Justine glanced at the watch strapped to her left wrist. "I don't know exactly. I got off work a little later than usual, then drove straight home. I'd say it's been at least an hour and a half."

"And how were they when you found them?"

Her brows lifted as he turned back to her. "How were they?" she repeated inanely. "They were fine. In fact, I'd say they're both in perfect health."

Roy's eyes slowly drifted over her white nurse's shift. "I wasn't asking about their medical condition. I want to know where they were. In the house, here on the floor?"

There was a thread of impudence in his voice, a sound that said he was just waiting, hoping, for her to make some sort of foolish remark. A second time. Justine suddenly wanted to slap him.

She tried to count to ten, but her mind wavered. By the time she reached five, her attention had returned to his face, the chiseled mouth and the hooded gray-blue eyes, the sandy hair curling around his ears and the back of his neck. She'd once showered that face with kisses, she remembered, threaded her fingers though his hair and held his head fast to her breast.

He'd made her heart beat fast and wild then. She'd never loved anyone the way she loved him, and now, after all this time, she was afraid she never would again. This man had ruined her chances of happiness, and he didn't even know it. Moreover, he didn't care.

Her nostrils flaring, she lifted her chin. "The babies were on the porch by the door. In a laundry basket."

"Where is the basket?"

"In the kitchen."

"I'd like to see it."

And she'd like to stuff it over his head, Justine thought. But the pistol strapped to his hips and the badge pinned to his breast reminded her of his authority in this county, even in this house. She didn't want to test it at this moment.

"Follow me," she told him.

Justine took him to the kitchen, where the basket was still sitting atop the table. Ignoring her, he looked inside.

"Was there any sort of note, anything inside other than this blanket?"

"The only things I found were four diapers, two bottles and two pacifiers."

He looked at Justine, his lips thinning with obvious disapproval. "And you've handled them all?"

"Of course. I had to change the babies, and I didn't want the formula to spoil. The two of them will eventually need to eat."

He lifted his hat from his head and raked his fingers through his hair. Justine couldn't help but notice that it was still thick and shiny.

"I don't suppose you thought about getting finger-prints?"

She dismissed his question with a wave of her hand. "I'm not stupid, Roy. I think you and I both know that whoever left these babies doesn't have a criminal record or have their fingerprints on file. It doesn't appear to me to be a crime committed by a repeated felon with a jail record. There's no motive or gain."

She was probably right, but that didn't make him like the fact that she'd tampered with evidence. Besides that, he was finding it damn hard to concentrate on anything but her.

He'd thought seeing her again would be easy. He'd thought he could look at her and not remember the passion that had once burned so briefly between them. But images of the past were blurring his vision, reminding him of the fool he'd been.

"How old do you think the babies are?" he asked after a moment.

"Five months, give or take."

He walked over to the screen door leading out to the courtyard. "Do you have any idea who they might belong to, or where they might have come from?"

"No. No idea."

He continued to look out at the courtyard, with its brick patio, its redwood lawn furniture and its huge pots of bright flowers. Rooms and a ground-level porch were built in a square around the small yard. Directly in front of him, on the south wall, a wrought-iron gate led outside, to the barns and stables.

From where Roy stood, he could see nothing out of the ordinary. He glanced at Justine. Her face was pale, and her fingers were nervously tracing a pattern on the edge of the laundry basket.

"Have you ever seen the twins before?"

"No."

His jaw tight, Roy looked away from her. "I need to take a look around the place. Do I have your permission, or should I drive back to Carrizozo and get a search warrant?"

Justine's lips parted as her eyes bored into the side of his darkly tanned face. "A search warrant? Do you think I had something to do with the twins appearing on the doorstep?"

He turned to face her. "I didn't say that."

"You didn't have to."

Roy frowned at her incredulous expression. "This is your home, Justine, your property. Not mine. If you don't want me on it, you have the legal right to see a search warrant. As a lawman—"

"You don't have to remind me you're the law of Lincoln County, Roy," she said dryly. "I'm well aware that you are."

So she thought he was cocky, just here to flaunt his authority in her face. Well, there were a lot of things Roy was thinking about her, too. But he wasn't going to voice them. The past was dead, and he wasn't going to give Justine Murdock the satisfaction of knowing how hard it had been for him to finally bury it.

Striding over to her, he looked down at her upturned face. "I'm glad you realize that, Justine."

Her nostrils flared as her eyes scanned his face, then settled on the firm line of his lips.

She realized a lot of things about him, Justine thought. That these past six years had not only lined his face and muscled his body, they had extinguished the light that once burned in his eyes. The smile that had always been so ready on his lips had totally disappeared. What had happened to the Roy Pardee she used to know?

"Go ahead. Do your search," Justine told him, her eyes drifting to a point over his shoulder. "You won't get any resistance from me."

Roy's lips twisted. Too bad she hadn't resisted his advances all those years ago. If she had, then maybe he wouldn't be feeling this awful, empty anger inside him now.

"Thank you. I'll try to be quick."

He left the room, and Justine immediately sagged against the table. Dear God, let this be over soon, she prayed. Let him be gone from here before her son and aunt returned.

Justine didn't know how long she stood there before the fussing of the babies called her back to the living room. Kneeling down on the pallet, she checked both their diapers. They were dry, so she patted their backs and tried talking to them. Neither the girl nor the boy seemed interested in what she had to say. Both simply chewed their fists and cried harder. Justine knew there was nothing left to do but heat their bottles and feed them.

By the time Roy returned from his search through the house and over part of the grounds, Justine was sitting on the floor with the babies, doing her best to balance bottles in each hungry mouth.

"Thank God you're back!" Before Roy could say anything, she picked up the boy and thrust him into his arms. "You can feed him while I take the girl."

Stunned, Roy looked helplessly at the baby in his arms. "I don't know anything about feeding a baby!"

Frowning at him, she cradled the redheaded girl in her arms. "Just put the nipple in his mouth and keep the bottle tilted up. He'll do the rest."

Roy awkwardly carried the boy and the bottle over to the couch and took a seat on the edge of the cushion. As soon as he offered the baby the nipple, the little tyke latched on to it like a hungry pup.

"I didn't come here to act as a temporary daddy," he muttered.

Temporary daddy. Justine's lips twisted with a grimace as she repeated the two words to herself. The man didn't look as if he'd be comfortable in that role, much less being a father in a permanent capacity.

"I know you didn't come here for this. But I can't handle two of them at the same time. And when a baby gets hungry, he doesn't care where he is or who he's with, he wants his dinner. Surely you know that."

Roy shot her a glare as the baby reached for the shiny badge pinned to the pocket of his khaki shirt.

"How would I know that? I've never had a child!"

He growled the question at Justine, and, if it was possible, her face went even whiter. I've never had a child. What was he saying? What about Marla, and the baby she and Roy had been expecting all those years ago? The questions roared through her head like a tornado.

Through offhand remarks of her father's, Justine had learned that Roy and Marla's marriage had ended and the woman had moved far away. At the time of the divorce, it had been rumored that Marla was pregnant, but Tom had never heard anything about a child being born and he hadn't wanted to appear nosy and ask Roy outright. Especially since the two of them had been divorced.

Down through the years, Justine had simply assumed the baby had been born and lived with its mother in another state. Now Roy was telling her he'd never had a child! What did it all mean?

Struggling to collect her thoughts, she said, "I— Well, I just figured you were probably a daddy by now."

Roy glanced down at the auburn-haired boy in his arms. The tiny fingers were doing their best to tug the sheriff's badge away from his shirt. Carefully he plucked the baby's hand away, only to have the stubby little fingers wrap tightly around his forefinger.

"Do I look like one?" he asked gruffly.

No, she thought, her teeth grinding together, Roy Pardee was the very image of a man who liked to make babies, not father them.

Ignoring his question, she asked, "Did you find anything outside?"

The baby was still clinging to his finger. It made him feel hemmed in, but needed. And that was a strange feeling for Roy. No one had ever really needed him. As a lawman, maybe. But not like this helpless little fellow in his arms.

"No. I need to talk to your sisters. When do you think they'll be in?"

Justine shrugged as she absently rocked the child in her arms. "By dark. Maybe later. Rose is probably out in one of the pastures checking on the cattle, and Chloe should have been down at the stables with the horses. You didn't see her?

"No. The barns and the stables were all empty."

Glancing down, Justine studied the little girl's round face, dimpled cheeks and soft red hair. "Do you think it was the parents that left these children here? I mean, how could someone do such a thing? If I hadn't come home when I had—" Shuddering at the thought, she shook her head. "With just a little motion, they could have turned that basket over. No telling what would have happened to them."

Roy could see that the idea of the babies being harmed alarmed her greatly. It bothered him, too. Still, he didn't think the person or persons who'd left the twins had meant to put their lives in jeopardy. "It's too early to say if it might have been one or both of the parents, or someone unrelated. The only thing that's clear to me is that whoever left them here meant for you or one of your family members to have them."

Justine's head swung back and forth. "But that's insane! Why would someone want me or my sisters to have their babies?"

Roy shrugged. "You're a nurse. Maybe someone knew that and believed you'd take good care of them."

Milk was dribbling from the corner of the baby's mouth.

Drawing a handkerchief from his pocket, Roy dabbed it away. With the bottle still in his mouth, the little boy grinned broadly and let out a happy goo.

Scowling, Roy jammed the damp handkerchief back in his pocket. Poor little guy, he thought grimly. He wasn't even aware that he'd been abandoned. He was too small to know about the pain of rejection. But Roy knew all about it, and even though the person or persons who'd left these babies behind might not have intended physical harm to them, they still needed to be strung up by the heels. Roy vowed then and there to track them down, no matter how long it took!

Across the room, Justine watched the dark, angry expression spread over Roy's face as he looked down at the baby in his arms. She couldn't believe what she was seeing. There was such hardness in his eyes and on his lips. Was the man totally heartless? Didn't he feel anything for the helpless child in his arms?

If it hadn't been for the girl still feeding in her arms, Justine would have ripped the baby away from him and ordered him out of the house. As it was, however, she was hardly in a position to vent her feelings to him.

But she would someday, Justine silently promised herself. Someday she'd let him know what a selfish, heartless man he really was.

From out of nowhere, hot moisture blurred her vision. She shut her eyes and swallowed at the unexpected rush of emotion. This wasn't like her to get teary and mad and vindictive. Normally she was a loving woman. But Roy Pardee, or the thought of him, had never left her feeling normal.

The sound of a vehicle caught both her and Roy's attention. Rising up in the rocking chair, Justine glanced out the window. Her heart immediately dropped to her stomach.

"It's my aunt," she told Roy.

He nodded.

Moments later, a screen door banged and the patter of racing feet on Spanish tile grew closer. Then, suddenly, the running footsteps stopped and Charlie, her five-year-old son, stood just inside the living groom, his wide blue eyes going from his mother and the baby in her arms to the strange man on the couch.

"It's all right, darling. You can come on in," Justine told him gently.

With a cautious eye on Roy, the boy scurried to Justine's side.

"Mommy, where did you get the baby? Who is that man? He's got a baby, too!"

Justine cast a glance at Roy. He was staring at her and Charlie, his eyes squinted to slits, his jaw rigid. She couldn't tell exactly what he was thinking, but it was quite clear that the appearance of her son wasn't pleasing to him. And suddenly she knew she'd been right all those years ago. She could stop beating up on herself, stop feeling guilty. Roy Pardee hadn't been father material then, and he wasn't now.

"Yes, honey. Mommy found the babies, and the sheriff has come to help find out where they belong."

Smiling with instant fascination, Charlie carefully touched the red fuzz of hair on the girl twin's head. "She has red hair like you, Mommy!"

Justine smiled at her son's observation. "She sure does. Now, will you go get Aunt Kitty? The sheriff would like to speak with her."

Charlie glanced curiously over at the man and the baby on the couch, then started toward the door. "Aunt Kitty had to go to the bathroom! I'll get her!"

Charlie raced out of the room. Once the boy was out of sight, Roy released a long breath he hadn't realized he'd been holding.

"You have a son?"

The sound of his low, gravelly voice caused Justine to

jerk ever so slightly. She looked up from the baby and over to him. There was an odd look of betrayal on his face. As though he knew... But no, she swiftly assured herself. He couldn't know anything. No one, not even her sisters, knew that Roy Pardee was Charlie's father.

Chapter Two

Justine's chin unconsciously tilted upward. "Yes. Charles is my son."

Of course, it had been obvious when the boy called her Mommy. But hearing Justine admit it out loud was like the blow of an ax to Roy.

His face like chipped granite, he said, "Someone told me you'd been engaged to be married, then later I heard the marriage had been called off. But I didn't know you'd had a child back then. Did you...ever get married?"

Roy hated himself for asking. He wanted to appear indifferent. He wanted to be totally disinterested, but he couldn't be. Justine Murdock had done something to him all those years ago. She'd shown him heaven and then shown him hell. She'd given him his first true love lesson. One that he'd never forget. There wasn't such a thing as real love.

"No. I've never been married," Justine admitted, then wondered what he could possibly be thinking. Let it be that she was a promiscuous woman. Anything would be better than the truth.

"You had the boy while you were in college."

It was a statement, not a question, but Justine found herself nodding at him anyway. She was determined to appear cool, no matter how much her insides were shaking with fear. "Being pregnant and going to school wasn't a picnic. I had to cut down on my classes and scrimp and save the money my parents sent me. But I managed to get through."

"So where is his father?"

She met his gaze, and her green eyes were unusually dull. "After I became pregnant with Charlie, he realized he didn't want to be a family man. He didn't even want to get married. So we—ended things, and since then he's been totally out of my life."

Roy wanted to tell her she'd been a fool to bear such a man's child, but at that moment a petite woman with short salt-and-pepper hair walked into the room. Justine's son was tagging close to her side.

"Charlie said I was wanted," Kitty said. "What's going on here?"

With the twin girl still in her arms, Justine got to her feet. "Roy, this is my aunt Kitty. She's my mother's sister. She came to live with us before our mother passed away."

"Nice to meet you, ma'am," Roy said, with a nod toward the older woman. "It seems that your niece found two babies on the porch when she came home from work. You wouldn't happen to know who they might belong to?"

Kitty's mouth formed a perfect O as she glanced from one baby to the other. "Land sakes no! You mean they were on the doorstep? Just like in the movies?"

"That's the way Justine described it."

Justine turned her eyes on him. "That's the way it was," she said crisply.

"Well! What do you think about that?" Kitty asked no one in particular. "I wish Lola and Tom were alive to see this."

Charlie ventured over to Roy, who'd just slipped the empty bottle from the boy twin's mouth.

"You have a badge," Charlie told him.

Roy looked at the boy. He had a stocky build, like his late grandfather Tom. His thick hair was light brown and fell in a straight bang across his forehead. Freckles dotted his broad-bridged nose and dimples dented both cheeks. He was an endearing child, and Roy couldn't help but somehow feel cheated that Justine had chosen to have some other man's baby.

"Yes, that's a badge," Roy told him.

"You have a gun, too," Charlie went on, his gaze on the pistol holstered to Roy's hip.

"That's right."

"Are you a policeman?"

"I'm a sheriff."

Charlie repeated the word. "What does a sheriff do?"

"He tells the other policemen what to do."

Charlie grinned and plopped down beside Roy on the couch. "So you're the boss."

In spite of everything, Roy found himself smiling back at Justine's son. "That's one way of putting it."

"Would you like for me to take the baby now, Mr. Pardee?" Kitty asked him.

"Thank you, ma'am." He handed the twin over to the older woman, and was instantly struck by the emptiness of his arms.

"He looks like the one you have, Mommy," Charlie said, pointing at the tiny boy in his aunt's arms. "Is that his sister?"

"Yes, honey. I expect they are brother and sister," Justine told him.

"I can't get over it," Kitty said as she strolled around the room like a doting grandmother. "Babies left on our ranch! Where do you think they came from?"

"I was hoping that you or Justine's sisters might have

some clues," Roy told the woman. "Are you certain you don't know anyone who's had twins in the past six months? An old friend or distant relative?"

Kitty thought for a moment, then shook her head. "My old friends are too old to have babies, and most of my relatives live here on the Bar M."

Sighing, Roy glanced at Charlie, who was sidled up to him the way a tomcat would a warm stove. The sight of the trusting child disturbed Roy almost as much as the sight of Justine.

Rising to his feet, he said, "Well, if neither of you can think of anything else, I'm going to get on the phone and find a place to take these babies tonight."

Roy headed out the door. Justine glanced at Kitty, then quickly placed the twin girl down on the pallet and followed him out on the porch.

Hearing her footsteps, Roy turned, his brows arched with speculation.

"Was there something else you wanted to tell me?" he asked.

Justine met his eyes, moistened her lips, then glanced away. "Just that there's no need for you to find a place for the babies to stay. We'd be happy to keep them here."

He didn't say anything, just kept gazing at her through narrowed eyes.

Justine heaved out a breath, then folded her arms across her breasts. "I love babies, but I wouldn't go so far to steal a pair of them, if that's what you're thinking."

"You don't know what I'm thinking," he said roughly.

And she didn't want to know, Justine thought hotly. "Well, think about this. There's not exactly a plethora of orphanages around here. As far as I know, there's not any. You probably know a few foster parents who'd be willing to take the babies in, but I doubt they would be any more capable than four grown women would be."

His gaze slanted downward from her face, to settle on the bulge of her breasts spilling over her folded arms.

"Don't forget to point out you're an experienced mother," he added sarcastically.

At that moment, Justine was certain she hated this long-legged man with hard blue eyes and an even harder mouth.

"Is there something wrong with being a mother?" she asked him challengingly.

Roy didn't know why he was behaving so churlishly. Just because seeing Justine again had thrown him off kilter, that didn't mean he lacked manners.

"No. There's nothing wrong with it," he said. Then with a tired sigh, he lifted his hat and combed his fingers through his hair.

The sun had set some minutes ago, and the sky over the ranch had turned dusky. The day had been a long one for Roy. He should be looking forward to going home, taking a hot shower and fixing himself a steak for supper. But not even the prospect of those things eased the weariness that had suddenly come over him.

"I suppose it will be all right for the babies to stay here tonight," he said after a moment. "I'll have someone from social services come out to get them tomorrow."

He stepped off the porch. Justine suddenly realized he was going to leave. "You're not going, are you?"

A faint smile touched his lips, but not his eyes. For one brief moment, Justine felt a sadness she didn't quite understand. She only knew that a long time ago, Roy had smiled at her. Really smiled. But she would never see that man again.

"There's not much more I can do here tonight, other than speaking with your sisters. And since they obviously weren't around when the babies were left, they may not know any more than your aunt. But just in case, I'll question them later. Until then, if any of you come up with something, let me know."

He took a step toward a Bronco with the sheriff's department seal painted on the side. Justine called after him.

"How long do you think it will take you to find out who did this?"

He glanced over his shoulder at her. "Not long," he said grimly.

"But you hardly have any evidence to work with."

"I've had less."

Behind Justine, the door opened and closed. She peered around to see Charlie skipping toward her.

"Mommy, I'm hungry. When are we gonna eat?"

Justine took her son by the shoulders and turned him back toward the door of the house. "Go get a graham cracker. Aunt Kitty and I will fix supper in a few minutes."

The child went back inside. Justine looked at Roy, and suddenly felt more awkward than she had since he first arrived. Maybe it was because he was leaving and she knew that she'd probably never see him again.

The idea should have relieved her, and it did, to a certain degree. But it also reminded her of how empty, how devastated, she'd felt when she lost him all those years ago. He'd been her first and only lover. Whether she wanted him to be or not, a part of him was still ingrained in her.

"Well, another hungry mouth to feed," she said, with a faint smile and a shrug. "I guess I'd better get to work."

Nodding, Roy turned and walked the remaining distance to his Bronco. He needed to get back to work, too. But he could feel her eyes on his back until he heard the door to the house shut.

Roy climbed into the vehicle and reached to start the motor. Before he could, his eyes were drawn to the house, and his fingers paused on the ignition keys. Through the living room window, he could see Justine bending down and planting a kiss on the top of her son's head. The boy took a bite of cracker, then offered it to his mother. She took a bite, then put her arm around the child and led him away from Roy's view.

Annoyed with himself for letting his attention stray once again to the family inside the house, Roy muttered a curse and started the engine. It was high time he got home.

Justine was helping her aunt prepare supper when Rose and Chloe returned to the house. Both sisters were instantly captivated by the twins and insisted on feeding them mashed bananas at the supper table.

"Aren't they the cutest things you've ever seen?" Chloe exclaimed as she scooped a spoonful of fruit into the boy's mouth. "What do you think we should call them?"

Justine glanced anxiously at her aunt then back to her younger sister. "Chloe, we can't name the babies. Remember what I told you earlier? Someone from social services will be out tomorrow to get them."

Chloe kissed the top of the boy's head, whose dark auburn hair just happened to match her own, then glanced adoringly at the girl sitting contentedly on Rose's lap.

"Oh, Justine, surely we can keep them until the real parents are found. And who knows? They might not be able to get them back. Not after dumping them like they did."

Justine sighed inwardly. She knew what these two babies probably meant to Chloe. At eighteen, an infection had scarred her reproductive organs and left her barren. Now, at twenty-three and with no chance of ever having a baby of her own, she probably saw the twins as two little angels sent from heaven.

But Justine knew it wasn't that way, and she didn't want Chloe or Rose to get attached to the babies, then go through the heartache of giving them up.

"Chloe," Justine began, "we don't know who left the children here. And I doubt—"

At twenty-eight, the chestnut-haired Rose was the oldest of the three sisters, and always the quiet one. But at this moment she chose to interrupt, making the other three women look at her with raised brows.

"If Sheriff Pardee allowed them to stay here tonight, perhaps he'll consider letting them stay until the case is solved."

"Yes!" Chloe seconded that idea with an eager yelp, then turned pleading eyes on Justine. "Justine, will you call and ask him?"

Justine glanced frantically at her two sisters. "*Me* ask him! Why me?"

"Well, you knew him from a long time ago," Chloe pointed out.

"I did?" Justine asked cautiously.

As far as she knew, no one in her family had known that she and Roy were together, as friends or anything more. At the time she became involved with Roy, he'd been dating Marla, his boss's daughter. But he'd assured Justine the relationship wasn't serious and he was trying to gradually break away from her without angering Marla or her father. So she'd agreed to keep their dating a secret. Now that secret was buried deep in her heart.

"We all went to the same high school," Rose reminded her.

"Oh—yes, I guess we did," Justine admitted with relief. "But he was three grades higher than me, and I never associated with the guy. Besides—"

Chloe butted in. "Justine, men take to you like ducks to water."

"Oh, please," Justine groaned. "I haven't even dated a man in a long time."

"Well," Rose said, her pretty face suddenly taking on a hard edge, "I'm sure not a femme fatale, and I'll not try to be."

As Justine glanced at her older sister, she realized she wasn't the only one who'd suffered because of a heartless man. Since her disastrous engagement ended nine years ago, Rose had shunned virtually all men.

"And you know how easily an arrogant man can rile me up," Chloe added. "Before I could bite my tongue, I'd be telling the sheriff to jump in the lake. Instead of wooing him to our way of thinking."

It was true Chloe had a feisty temper. She got along with her horses far better than she did with men. Still, it went against everything inside Justine to ask Roy for anything.

"I don't know why you two are doing this to me," Justine said wearily.

"Because you'd have a far better chance of persuading the sheriff than Rose or I," Chloe insisted. "Come on, say you'll do it. Please!"

If her sisters only knew, Justine thought sickly. What would they think if she told them that Sheriff Pardee was Charlie's father?

Closing her eyes, Justine pinched the bridge of her nose and shook her head. "We're already shorthanded here on the ranch. You and Rose work like dogs from sunup to sundown. How are you going to take care of two demanding babies?"

"I'll manage through the day," Kitty spoke up. "Charlie is big enough to fetch things for me. Besides, since Tom died, the house seems so quiet and empty. The babies will put a little life back into things around here."

Justine groaned. Rose smiled and nodded, while Chloe clapped her hands together.

Chloe pressed on. "That's right. The babies will help take our minds off all the problems we've been having lately. And it will be good for Charlie to have other children around."

Justine let out a long sigh. How could she say no, when the whole family was counting on her? "It could only be temporary," she pointed out.

"Temporary is a start," Rose said quietly.

Justine tossed her hands resignedly up in the air. "All right, okay. I'll call him. But don't get your hopes up. Sheriff Pardee doesn't strike me as a warmhearted man." In fact, Justine didn't think he had a heart at all, but she couldn't express that thought to her sisters. Not without raising some eyebrows. As far as they knew, he was just an old acquaintance, not the only man she'd ever loved.

Normally, Justine helped with cleaning the kitchen after the evening meal, but this time, both sisters shooed her out of the room.

"We'll take care of this mess. You go call the sheriff," Chloe told her.

Knowing her sisters wouldn't let her put it off any longer, Justine walked down to her bedroom and shut the door. If she had to talk to Roy, she wanted to do it in private.

As a nurse, Justine had been schooled to remain calm in a crisis. She'd seen people broken and bleeding and dangerously close to death, but she'd forced herself to be collected and focus on her job. Yet just the act of dialling Roy's number had her hand shaking and her breaths coming in shallow little jerks. It wasn't right that one man could have so much of an effect on her, she thought with self-disgust. Especially when he'd been out of her life for years now.

It rang four times, and Justine was on the verge of hanging up when he answered.

"Sheriff Pardee."

"Roy."

He knew instantly that it was Justine. No other woman had ever said his name quite like she did. He closed his eyes and gripped the receiver.

"Yes."

"This is Justine."

"I know."

Her shaky legs forced her to take a seat on the edge of the bed. "I—I'm calling about the twins."

"I didn't think you were calling to ask me for a date," he said dryly.

Her nostrils flared as she closed her eyes. She wished she could get her hands around his throat! No—she instantly changed her mind. She didn't want to touch him. Ever! If she did, she didn't know what she'd do. Kiss him? Claw him? Break down in tears? She wasn't going to test herself.

"I don't know how you ever won the sheriff's election," she muttered.

To Justine's amazement, he chuckled. The sound sent little shivers of nerves tumbling through her stomach.

"I won it because the majority of the people in Lincoln County like and trust me."

Even if you don't. Justine could hear the unspoken words hovering on the line between them.

Knowing she'd never get anywhere with him if she allowed her temper to get the better of her, she said, "I heard you got ninety percent of the vote. Are you sure you had an opponent?"

"Somebody mentioned there was another guy running for the job. I didn't notice."

His cockiness had Justine rolling her eyes. "Well, I'm glad to hear you're so liked and well-thought-of around here," she said, "because I'm going to...ask a favor of you."

Roy had been lying back in his leather recliner, but now his boots hit the floor with a loud thud. In his wildest dreams, he'd never expected Justine Murdock to want or need any sort of help from him. He didn't know whether to tell her to go to hell, or silently thank God. In fact, for years now Roy had never been quite able to decide if he hated Justine or loved her.

"A favor," he repeated, his voice gone husky. "What kind?"

She drew in a shaky breath. "It's about the twins. Do you think it might be possible for us...I mean, my sisters and me...to keep them here until...you locate the real parents?"

"Why would you want to do that? I'm sure you and your family have plenty to keep you busy besides two demanding babies."

"Of course we do. But my sisters are infatuated with the babies, and since...Daddy's death, well, I think it would be good for all of us to have them around."

Roy knew that Justine had been very close to her mother and father. She was probably still grieving over Tom's death. If the babies could help ease the ache, what the hell, he thought. Even though she'd made his life miserable, that didn't mean he wanted to rub salt in her wounds.

"You don't have to sell me on the idea, Justine. I know I can trust the twins' welfare to you and your family."

She couldn't believe he'd so readily agreed to her request, and for a moment she didn't know what to say.

"Justine? Isn't that what you wanted to hear?"

"I— Uh, yes," she finally managed to answer. "Is that all we have to do? Is your permission enough to keep them here?"

"Legally, no. I'll have to get a court order from Judge Richards. But he and I are good friends. He'll go along with my feelings on the matter."

"That's all there is to it?"

"You sound surprised."

She was. She'd expected Roy to resist everything about the idea. Now, because of who he was and what he was, he was going to make it legally possible for her family to keep the babies. She didn't know what to think.

"I guess I expected it to be a lot more complicated."

"Well, since it's only a temporary situation, there's not

that much legal red tape.'' He paused, then asked, ''Justine, you do understand that once this case comes to some sort of end, you'll have to give the babies up?''

''Yes. I understand. I don't know if my sisters will. But I do.''

''Then, for their sake, you'd better remind them.''

''I will. And thank you, Roy.''

She thought she heard him sigh. ''Good night, Justine.''

''Good night.''

Slowly, Justine replaced the receiver, then stared blankly at the floor. After a moment, tears blurred her eyes. She wiped at them viciously and tried to swallow away the tightness in her throat.

She didn't know what was the matter with her. Her sisters were going to be very happy, and Roy had been almost nice to her. There was no reason for her to get emotional. No reason at all.

A light knock sounded on the bedroom door. Justine quickly wiped her eyes again. ''Come in.''

Stepping into the room, Chloe looked hopefully at Justine. ''Did you call the sheriff?''

Justine nodded. ''We can keep the babies.''

Chloe gasped with joy. ''Oh, Justine, that's wonderful! See, I knew you could persuade him!''

Justine sighed. ''Believe me, Chloe, there was no persuading to it.''

Chloe eased down on the bed beside her sister. ''You don't sound very excited about it.'' She peered anxiously at Justine. ''Have you...been crying?''

Justine quickly shook her head. ''No, of course not. I think—I might be coming down with a cold. The clinic has been full of sniffling people.''

''Why don't you go to bed early tonight?'' Chloe suggested as she rose to her feet. ''Rose and I will see to the babies. She's gone up in the attic right now, to see if she can find our old baby bed and playpen. I'd better go see if she needs some help.''

"What's Charlie doing?"

Chloe laughed. "He's playing with the twins. He thinks those babies are the grandest things to come along since dump trucks and tractors.''

Justine smiled wanly. She'd never wanted Charlie to be an only child. But time had a way of passing on. Now he was five, and she was no closer to marrying and adding to her family than she had been when she gave birth to him.

Rising from her seat on the bed, she said, "I'm glad he's taken to the twins. But right now it's getting close to his bedtime. I'd better go coax him into the bathtub.''

As the two sisters walked down the wide hallway, toward the living room, Chloe slung her arm around Justine's shoulders.

"Do you realize how lucky you are to have a child, Justine?''

In spite of Roy, and the fact that Charlie was growing up without a father, Justine was very aware of the precious blessing her son was to her. She wished with all her heart that Chloe could have the chance to be a mother.

Slipping her arm around her younger sister's waist, she gave her an affectionate squeeze. "I realize it every day.''

Chloe sighed. "You know, there has to be a reason for those babies showing up here on the ranch.''

"I'm sure there is. We just don't know what it is yet.''

"Well, I think they're a gift from God. He took Daddy from us, so he's given us the babies to fill his place in the family.''

Justine glanced anxiously at her sister. "Chloe, Roy wanted me to remind you and Rose that keeping the babies on the ranch is only a temporary thing. You'll have to give them up eventually. You know that, don't you?''

"You wouldn't give Charlie up, would you?''

She tried to imagine Roy filing for custody of his son,

and found the image so frightening that she instantly put it out of her mind. "Not for anyone or anything. But, Chloe, Charlie is mine. There's a difference."

"Well, those twins are going to be mine. You just wait and see," she said.

Justine didn't argue with her sister. Instead, she silently prayed that Roy would soon solve the case.

The next morning, Justine was taking a much-needed coffee break on a little bench outside the clinic building when she saw Roy walking up the sidewalk toward her.

He was dressed as he had been yesterday, in jeans, boots and a khaki shirt. Justine couldn't help but notice his long legs and lean waist, the width of his broad shoulders beneath the close-fitting fabric. He was a very sexy man. But sex was all he had to offer a woman. She knew that better than anyone.

"How did you know where I worked?" Justine asked as he came to a halt in front of her.

A faint smile touched his lips, as though he found her question amusing. "I'm the sheriff, remember? I can find out most anything I need to know."

Not everything, she promised herself as her thoughts went to their son. He could search all he wanted to, but there was no way he was going to find out he'd fathered Charlie. Unless she told him. And right now, she couldn't see herself ever doing that.

"What did you need to see me about?" she asked, her fingers curled tightly around the foam-cup of coffee in her hands.

He pulled a piece of paper out of his shirt pocket and unfolded it. "I need your signature on this before I take it back to Judge Richards."

She accepted the paper from him and read it carefully. Once Justine was satisfied that she understood it, she slipped a pen from a pocket of her shift and quickly signed her name.

Handing it back to him, she asked, "Do you have any new information about the twins?"

He pushed the legal document into his pocket. "No. Other than that no children fitting the twins' description have been listed as missing in the state in the past twenty-four hours."

"Does that surprise you?"

He watched Justine sip her coffee. The morning was cool but clear. The bright sunlight caught her red hair and turned the wavy tendrils to molten bronze. She was still by far the most beautiful woman he'd ever know, and he wondered what had happened between her and Charlie's father. Why hadn't the man married her? Or had it been Justine's choice to end their engagement?

"Not really," he said in answer to her question. "Like I said, whoever left the twins intended your family to have them. They're not going to go to the police. Unless they have a change of heart."

"Then how do you plan to start an investigation without anything to go on?"

"I already have. My deputies are out now, questioning everyone and anyone up and down the streets of town to see if the twins were seen around here yesterday. It could be they traveled through Ruidoso before going on to the Bar M."

Ruidoso wasn't a particularly large metropolis, but it was a heavily traveled tourist town. Thousands of people came to see the horse races at Ruidoso Downs, shop the unique little stores lining the highways and simply enjoy the sight of the cool, beautiful mountains. How could anyone remember one set of babies, when they saw tourists with babies every day? Justine wondered.

"That's another thing that puzzles me," Justine mused

aloud. "How did this person or persons know where the ranch was?"

"Because they know you, or at least know of you. That's why you and your family need to rack your brains. You might come up with something or someone."

Her break time nearly over, Justine rose to her feet and brushed at the wrinkles in her straight skirt. "Of course, we'll try. Now I have to get back inside."

Roy needed to get to work himself. But he was reluctant to leave just yet. Last night, after Justine called, he'd spent hours thinking about her, the way she'd looked and sounded, and the way he'd felt upon learning that she'd loved some other man enough to have his child. He hadn't expected to feel anything like regret. Six years ago, when he became involved with her, he hadn't been ready for marriage or children. So why did it hurt so much to think of her turning to another man?

"How long have you worked here?"

Surprised by the personal question, she slanted him a glance from beneath her lashes. "Since before Mother died seven months ago."

He grimaced. "I was sorry to hear about her passing."

He sounded sincere, and somehow that made it harder for Justine to remain callous toward him. She knew that Roy had lost his mother long before he was grown. His father had died in a hunting accident when Roy was only a teenager. He understood what it was like to lose a parent.

"I moved back to the Hondo valley to be with her and nurse her while I could."

His eyes searched her face. "And you stayed because...?"

She met his gaze. Was he thinking the reason was him? No, surely not. It should be obvious. She'd been home a year and half, and she'd carefully kept her distance from him.

"Mother's death made me realize how much I needed to

be with my family, and how much Charlie needed them, too.''

He glanced at the ground and shifted uncomfortably. ''Now, you've lost your father. That must have been quite a blow.''

''I think you know how much of a blow. You lost your father, too.''

He glanced up, and for a split second, Justine saw naked pain in his eyes, but it was gone just as swiftly and he was back to being the steely-eyed sheriff of Lincoln County.

''You remember that?'' he asked lowly.

He seemed surprised, and Justine couldn't understand why. True, their time together hadn't been that long. Two months, at the most. But during those weeks, she'd grown so very close to him. She'd learned all about his growing-up years, his hopes and disappointments, his dreams for the future. How could he think she had forgotten anything about him?

''Of course I remember. He was hunting elk up in the mountains near Cimarron and fell from a cliff.''

''I guess you do remember.''

Too much, Justine thought. Far too much. She turned down the sidewalk heading back to the entrance of the building, then paused awkwardly, a few steps away from him.

''I should thank you again for your help with the twins. I'm sure it would have been impossible for us to keep them if you hadn't intervened on our behalf. Chloe and Rose are beside themselves.''

Being the sheriff, Roy often received thanks from the people he was able to help. Yet a thank-you coming from Justine was something entirely different. He didn't want to be touched by it, but he was. He didn't want to be drawn to her beauty, but he was. More than that, he didn't want to think of her as his lover. In the past or the present. But he was. And he didn't know how to stop it.

"I'll be out at the ranch again this evening," he said without preamble.

Surprised, Justine looked at him. "For what?"

"Remember, I still need to talk to your sisters. I'd appreciate it if you'd tell them to be there. And I'd like to talk to you some more, too."

Her heart began to thud rapidly. "About the twins?"

One corner of his mouth curled mockingly. "What else?"

What else indeed, she thought, as heat colored her face. "All right. We'll be there."

He touched his finger to the brim of his Stetson, then turned and walked away.

Justine watched him until he was out of sight, then forced herself to go back inside to work. But forcing him out of her mind was another matter.

Chapter Three

That evening, when Justine got home from work, she scraped her hair back into a ponytail, donned a pair of old, faded jeans, a worn chambray work shirt and tennis shoes with paint splotches on the toes.

When Roy Pardee showed up, he was going to see that enticing him was the last thing on her mind, Justine assured herself as she walked down to the kitchen.

As she stepped into the room, Kitty looked up from her task at the cabinet. "What are you going to do, clean the attic?" the woman asked, her eyes running over Justine's grubby clothes.

"No. Just getting comfortable," Justine said offhandedly, then walked over to where the twins were seated, in two high chairs. Bibs were tied around their necks, and damp vanilla-wafer crumbs were scattered across the trays in front of them.

"Where did the high chairs come from?" Justine asked.

"Rose found one in the attic, and Vida brought the other one over this morning," Kitty said. Vida was an old friend of hers, who lived a few miles down the road, toward Picacho. "Her grandbabies have all grown out of the high-chair stage, and she said she wouldn't be needing it."

"She knew about the twins being here?"

"I told her last night on the phone. But I think the whole Hondo Valley must know by now. The telephone has been ringing all day."

Justine tweaked both babies' cheeks with thumb and forefinger. "I guess it would be impossible to keep the news from traveling. Especially with Roy's deputies asking questions all over town."

Kitty turned her attention back to the cookbook lying open on the cabinet counter. "How do you know this?"

"Roy told me," Justine answered. "He came to the clinic this morning to have me sign a legal document about keeping the twins."

"So that part of it is already settled?"

Justine walked over to the coffeemaker sitting on the small breakfast bar. "Yes. It's all legal now. We keep the twins until Roy finds the parents."

Kitty looked up from the cookbook. "Sounds like Sheriff Pardee works fast. But, to be honest, I don't really know how he plans to find who the twins belong to. What does the man have to go on?"

Justine filled a pottery mug full of coffee and took a cautious sip. "Frankly, I don't know. But he seems confident. By the way, he's coming back out to the ranch this evening to speak with Rose and Chloe." Justine refused to add herself to that list. "Did I tell you?"

Glancing over her shoulder, Kitty frowned at her niece. "You knew the sheriff was coming out to the ranch and you dressed in that getup?"

"What do you mean? Roy isn't coming out here to see what I'm wearing," she said with faint irritation.

"Why, Justine," Kitty scolded lightly, "I didn't imply anything of the sort. It's just that you're usually so conscious of your appearance. And Sheriff Pardee is a very good-looking man. Single, too."

Justine wasn't surprised at the direction Kitty's mind had taken. Her aunt was always trying to find husbands for all three of her nieces. "I heard he was divorced."

"Hmm... I think that's true. Someone—maybe it was Vida—said he used to be married to the past sheriff's daughter. But the marriage only lasted two or three months. Strange, isn't it, two people go to all the trouble of getting married and then can't stay together for more than twelve weeks."

Justine tried not to appear shocked as she gazed at her aunt. Two months after she left Roy and went back to college in Las Cruces, Roy had tried to call her several times. Each time, she'd refused to talk to him. Had he and Marla already divorced by then? She didn't know why it should matter to her now, but it did.

"I wonder what ever happened to Marla?" Justine asked more to herself than Kitty.

Kitty leaned her hip against the cabinet and tapped a finger against her thumb. "You knew his wife?"

Justine nodded, but didn't say more. Since she returned home a year and a half ago, she'd deliberately refrained from asking her father or any of her old acquaintances anything about Roy. For one thing, she didn't want to arouse any sort of suspicion about Roy Pardee and herself. And for another, she'd always told herself she didn't care what had happened in his life once she went back to college.

Kitty spoke up, totally unaware of Justine's spinning thoughts. "Well, apparently the woman wasn't what the sheriff expected in a wife, because they split the blanket before it ever got warm."

And Justine could only wonder why. Was that what he'd been wanting to tell her when he called her at NMU all those years ago? That he and Marla were finished? And what about the baby Marla had been expecting? He'd said he'd never been a father. Had the woman suffered a miscarriage?

Oh, none of it mattered now, she wearily told herself. What had happened in the past couldn't change the way things were now.

"That's his business, Kitty. Not ours."

Before the older woman could reply, Justine carried her coffee out through the screen door and across the small courtyard. In one corner, Charlie was playing in the sandpile her father had built for his grandson before he died.

Smiling at the precious sight, Justine sat down beside her son and picked up a small road grader. "May I play, too?"

"Sure, Mommy." He pointed to a long trench he'd dug in the sand. "See, this is the Hondo River, and this is our house over here."

"And we need to have a bridge to cross to the other side," Justine observed. "Maybe we can find a few twigs to use for logs."

Twenty minutes later, Justine was admiring the miniature ranch she'd helped Charlie construct when the screen door leading out from the kitchen softly banged closed. Glancing up, she saw Roy sauntering slowly toward them.

Before Justine could say a word, Charlie jumped to his feet and went to meet him.

"You're the sheriff," he said, smiling up at the tall man with the black Stetson and the steel-blue eyes. "Did you come here to arrest us?"

Roy had never felt comfortable with young children. He'd never been around them much, and he didn't know what they were capable of talking about or how their minds worked. Yet something about this sturdy little boy of Justine's was different. For some reason, he felt attuned to him.

"Do you know what *arrest* means?" he asked the child.

Charlie nodded vigorously. "Yep. Aunt Kitty told me

that's what sheriffs do. They arrest people who do bad things and take them to jail.''

His expression serious, Roy said, "Your aunt Kitty is right. Have you done something bad?"

Charlie wagged his head back and forth. "No. If I do something bad, Mommy won't let me ride the horses with Aunt Chloe."

Sounded like Justine knew the right button to push to keep her son in line, Roy thought. "Then I'm not going to arrest you and take you to jail. You like to ride horses?"

Charlie's blue eyes lit up. "Yeah! I have a painted pony named Thundercloud."

"Can he run like the wind?"

Charlie grinned. "When Aunt Chloe rides him he goes really, really fast. But Mommy won't let me run him yet. She says I need to be six, and then I can take him on the galloping track."

"Sounds like you have something to look forward to," Roy told the boy.

"Charlie is like his Aunt Chloe. He has a great love affair with horses," Justine said as she walked up to the two of them.

Roy looked at her. "And what about you?"

Justine didn't want to get involved in small talk with this man. He'd caused her so much pain that she still, after all these years, wasn't able to forgive him. But since Charlie was present, Justine didn't want to appear short or impolite.

"I love horses. I just don't sleep, eat and breathe them, as my sister does," she said, her eyes meeting his, then glancing away.

"Kitty tells me Rose and Chloe went into town earlier."

Justine nodded. "To get a few things for the babies. Clothes, diapers, bottles and such. I'm sure they'll be back any time now. Chloe doesn't want the horses to go five minutes past their regular feeding time. She says it upsets their digestion, not to mention their nerves."

"I don't behave too well when I'm hungry, either."

Justine didn't think a full stomach could help Roy's at-titude. In fact, she was beginning to wonder what it would take to make the man smile more often.

At that moment, Kitty appeared in the open doorway behind them. "Sheriff Pardee," she called through the screen door. "The girls are back from town now, if you'd like to come in and speak with them."

"I'll be right there." He turned and headed toward the house. To Justine's surprise, Charlie followed behind him. She opened her mouth to call him back, then closed it just as quickly. Not allowing her son to go into the house would look odd. Besides, being around Roy for a few minutes wasn't going to harm him. Charlie was fascinated with the sheriff, not the man, she assured herself.

With the two of them gone, Justine decided to walk down to the stables and feed the horses. Roy might keep Chloe and Rose tied up for several minutes, and she knew both her sisters would enjoy a little extra time with the babies.

The stables were built on a sloping hill at the foot of the mountain. Several yards to the northwest, where the land flattened out to become valley floor, a plowed circle of track covered a half-mile distance.

Justine had seen her father stand many a time at the edge of the track, watching proudly as Chloe galloped his race-horses. He would be there no more, Justine thought sadly. And she was beginning to wonder how much longer they would be able to hold on to the racing stock. It was very expensive to keep a stable of horses, and since their father's death, they'd been faced with one debt after another. But there was always the possibility that one of the animals would win them a chunk of money. At least Chloe liked to think so.

Justine was filling the last hay bag with alfalfa when Roy entered the long barn. Determined to ignore her pounding heart, she leaned against the door of the stall and waited while he approached her.

"What are you doing down here?" she asked, annoyed that her voice had come out husky, rather than in the cool tone she'd been hoping for.

He didn't smile at her, but when his eyes met hers, they didn't seem nearly as hard as they had yesterday. Or was she only imagining that they had softened?

"I wanted to talk to you, remember?"

She'd been hoping he would forget. "I knew my sisters were busy, so I decided to do the feeding for them." Her eyes slipped over his face. "Did they have any helpful information?"

Roy shook his head. "No. All of you say there's no one out there that you know who would leave babies on the Bar M's doorstep."

Justine made a helpless gesture with her hand. "There isn't anyone we know. Look, Roy, all our friends and acquaintances live around here. They're the same people you know."

"What about Charlie's father?"

Justine's heartbeat went from fast to runaway. "Wh-what about Charlie's father?"

Frowning, Roy looped his thumbs over his belt. "Obviously he isn't from around here. Perhaps he had something to do with this?"

Justine was suddenly thinking of the old adage that one lie always calls for another. But in this case, she couldn't come out with the truth. Not now! Roy hadn't wanted a family back when Charlie was conceived, and judging by his single status now, he still didn't want one.

"There's no chance of that," she said curtly.

"How do you know?"

Justine frowned. "I just know. He—he doesn't have a wife or children. And he has nothing to do with my life now. He...doesn't want anything to do with it."

"You seem very certain of that."

Justine suddenly wondered if he was asking these questions because of the twins, or was merely using them as an excuse to pry into her life away from Hondo.

"I am certain."

She moved her eyes from his and fixed her gaze on the far end of the stables. She didn't want to keep looking at him. She was afraid that if she did, he'd be able to see the secrets she was hiding.

"Well, it's my job to ask these things. I'm not really trying to find out about your old lovers."

Her old lovers. Justine would have laughed if the whole thing wasn't so heartbreaking. Roy was the first and only lover she'd ever had. What would he think if he knew that? she wondered wildly.

"No, I don't expect you are," she said wryly.

Roy hadn't come down here to the stables to hash out the past with her. But as his eyes wandered over her face, the tender line of her jaw, the curve of her cheeks, the lush fullness of her lips, he couldn't help but want to know many things. Most of all, why he'd lost her.

"I would like to know one thing."

The quietness of his voice tugged her eyes back to his face. She couldn't read his stoic expression, but it hardly made any difference. Just seeing the chiseled lines of his face, the gray-blue of his eyes, made her remember how it had been to touch him, love him.

Before she could stop it, her mind went back to the day she and Roy had met. She'd been driving home during a semester break from college when, just north of Alamogordo, one of her tires suddenly blew. She'd been struggling to loosen the lug nuts when a patrol car pulled up behind her. The young deputy inside had been Roy, and by the time he'd changed the tire, she'd already agreed to meet him later in Ruidoso. The attraction between them had been instantaneous and overwhelming, and from that very day, Roy Pardee had changed her life.

"One thing?" she asked quietly, forcing her mind back to the present.

Roy closed the three steps between them, and Justine's breathing stopped as he placed his thumb beneath her chin and tilted her face up to his.

"Why did you leave? Why did you go without saying one word? Not even *goodbye?*"

Her green eyes grew wide, her lips parted. "My Lord, Roy, what would you have had me do?"

His face contorted with confusion and anger. "Come to me. Talk to me. I don't think that would have been asking too much."

Bitterness hardened her eyes and twisted the soft lines of her face. "You had no right to ask me anything. You got Marla pregnant while professing to love me!"

He looked sincerely surprised. "She told you that?"

The rage Justine had felt at him back then begged to be let loose now. It was all she could do to keep from screaming, beating his chest with her fists.

"Of course she told me," she said cuttingly. "You didn't seem to be able to."

Justine had never seen a look such as the one that suddenly spread over Roy's face. Hate, anger, regret and pain all mixed to contort his features into a feral snarl.

"Why would I want to tell you a lie?"

Her senses were so scattered by his nearness, she hardly knew what he was saying. But she did latch on to one word, and she repeated it in a blank question. "Lie? What are you trying to say?"

"I'm not trying to say anything. I *am* saying it."

He dropped his hold on her chin, then wiped a hand over his face. "What the hell..." he muttered. "It doesn't mean anything now."

Justine should have let it go at that. But she couldn't.

His words and his touch had inflamed her. She had to know what happened with him and Marla.

"If you didn't want to lie to me, why didn't you tell me about Marla—that she was pregnant with your child?"

Her question came out in a heated rush. Roy stared at her face, seeing the outrage there, and realized that she'd gone through all these years believing the worst of him.

"Because I didn't know anything about it."

Somewhere in the back of Justine's mind, she knew the best thing for her to do would be to leave the stables and never look back. But the years she spent away from her home and family had been the blackest of her life. She'd been young and alone and heartbroken, and this man had done it to her. She needed to know why.

"Sure," she said, her voice heavy with sarcasm. "The next thing you'll be telling me is that you never had sex with the woman."

"No. I did have sex with Marla," he admitted, with a rueful twist to his lips. "But it was before you and I became involved."

"How convenient. Did this happen hours before you asked me out on a date? Or can you narrow it down to minutes?"

"You're infuriating." He gritted out the words between clenched teeth. "You know I'd been trying to break up with Marla. I hadn't touched her in that way for weeks!"

"And you're disgusting to think I'd actually believe you! I'm not that same twenty-year-old you charmed and seduced."

He grabbed her by the shoulders, his fingers digging into the soft flesh of her arms. "Then believe this! Marla was never pregnant. She lied to you and she lied to me!"

His words knocked the wind from her, and she went limp against the wooden stall door. "She said—" Justine broke off as shock and regret swirled through her. "Marla told me she was carrying your child, and if I didn't believe her,

I could ask her doctor. She said I was standing in the way of you two getting married. She loved you and wanted to give her child your name. She said if I was any kind of woman at all, I'd leave you and the Hondo Valley for good.''

"Marla never loved anyone but herself," Roy said tightly.

She lifted accusing eyes to his. "You married her!"

"Only because she was carrying my child. At least I believed she was. And even though I didn't love her, I wanted my child to have a name. I didn't want it to be born a bastard.''

How ironic, Justine thought sickly. He'd wanted to do the honorable thing. Yet his son had been born a bastard anyway. How could she tell him that? She couldn't! He could never know that Charlie was his child!

"Can you understand the situation I was in, Justine?" he asked, jolting her straying thoughts back to the present. "Marla's father was the sheriff and my boss. He respected me. The whole town did. I couldn't ignore my responsibilities. But you wouldn't let me tell you any of this. You left without a word.''

Justine felt sick and defeated. Stepping away from his grasp, she turned her back to him. "What could you have really said, Roy? You chose her rather than me. End of story.''

"But it wasn't the end of the story," he said. "A few weeks after we were married, it became obvious to me that Marla wasn't pregnant. I was furious. I wanted to kill her. I knew she'd made up the whole thing to get you out of the picture.''

"Well, it worked," she said bitterly.

Roy sighed. "After we divorced, I called you to tell you what had happened. I tried several times, but you wouldn't talk to me.''

Pain spread from the middle of her chest up to her throat.

"I didn't want to talk to you. I knew you'd married Marla. And as far as I was concerned, it was all over between us."

Moving behind her, he placed his hands on top of her shoulders. To her disgust, his touch burned through her shirt.

"What would you have done if you'd know the truth about Marla?" he asked quietly, all the anger draining from his voice.

What *would* she have done? Justine asked herself. Would she have told him she was pregnant? He'd already married one woman out of obligation. Would it have eased her heart to be the second? She didn't think so.

Twisting her head around, she looked up at him. The moment her eyes connected with his blue ones, she felt her heart breaking all over again.

"You weren't ready to settle down to family life then," she said. "You told me that more than once. And I had my education to get. It's probably for the best that I didn't know."

"Best for whom—you?" he asked. "It must have been. You didn't waste any time finding another man."

She could hear accusation in his voice, yet she couldn't even defend herself, she realized. She couldn't tell him that he'd been the only man in her life without giving away her secret. She'd had to tell her family, everyone back in Hondo, that she'd gotten engaged to a college student, but he'd dropped her after she became pregnant. It had been the only thing she could think of to save face for herself, her baby, and perhaps even Roy.

"I had to get on with my life, Roy."

"And pretty damn quick, too, wasn't it? You'd hardly been gone a month when I heard you'd gotten engaged. Why didn't you marry Charlie's father?" he asked sharply.

Justine felt as though his hands were on her heart, rather than her shoulders, twisting and crushing what little was left of it.

"It turned out he didn't want me nearly as much as he thought he did. When he found out Charlie was on the way, he left me high and dry." Which was true enough, she thought sickly. Roy had left her for Marla. The other woman had been more important to him. "I guess I wasn't as lucky as Marla."

He didn't say anything, and Justine could only wonder if he was satisfied now. Had dredging up the past relieved him from some sort of guilt? The question very nearly made her snort out loud. What are you thinking, Justine? she asked herself. Roy Pardee never felt guilty about anything.

"Justine," he began softly, "I didn't want things—"

Justine couldn't stand any more. She didn't want to hear how it should have been, or could have been, if Marla hadn't chosen to tear them apart with her lies.

"I don't want to hear it," she said. Then, twisting away from his grasp, she hurried down the alleyway of the huge horse barn.

Roy caught up to her in three strides and took hold of her upper arm. His angry face bore down on hers. "Is that the only way you know how to deal with things? Walk away from them?"

Her teeth grinding together, Justine glared at him. "I don't have any 'things' to deal with. As far as I'm concerned, the past is just that. The past. I didn't ask you to come down here and—"

Her words, her touch, inflamed him, made him forget everything but the need to have her in his arms again.

With a small jerk of his hand, she tumbled against his chest. "You didn't ask for this, either," he muttered, then brought his lips roughly down on hers.

Outraged, Justine stiffened and pushed her fist against his chest. He didn't relent, his mouth continued its hot, hungry foray. And then, suddenly, stopping him wasn't nearly as important as simply hanging on.

Without her even knowing it, her hands spread open against his shoulders, and her lips parted. He tasted of promised heat and mindless ecstasy. It would be so easy to let herself want him again, need him again.

The road her thoughts had taken shocked her back to the reality of what she was doing. With a great mustering of strength, she twisted out of his embrace and backed away from him.

Her breast heaving, she glared at him. "You shouldn't have done that."

His top lip curled with mockery. "You and I have done a lot of things we shouldn't have. But kissing wasn't one of them."

"Get out!" she screamed. "I never want to see you again!"

Her anger caused a dry grin to spread across his face. "And what will you do if you see me again? Run away to Las Cruces? Find another man to cool that womanly fire of yours?"

She desperately wanted to slap him, but the fear that he might arrest her for assaulting a law officer stopped her. She didn't know Roy Pardee anymore. He was liable to do anything, she told herself.

"Believe me, when I go looking for another man, he won't have a badge on his chest and a gun on his hip!"

Roy looked pointedly down at himself. "I guess it's a good thing I keep these on—until I go to bed, that is."

If her eyes had been daggers, she would already have stabbed him to death. "You helped my sisters get temporary custody of the twins, but that doesn't mean I have to listen to this!"

His expression went flat. "Well, you won't have to listen to any more tonight, because I'm leaving."

"Good!"

He stepped past her and started toward the large open door at the east end of the barn. Before he reached it, he paused and glanced over his shoulder at her. She was watching him, her jaw clenched and her hands fisted at her sides.

"See you later," he told her.

"No, I won't. I don't plan on ever seeing you again."

A taunting smile lifted the corners of his lips. "We both know better than that."

A half hour passed before Justine was collected enough to return to the house. In front of her family, she pretended that everything was normal, that nothing out of the ordinary had happened between her and Roy down at the stables.

But later that night, when she went to bed, she could no longer keep up the pretense. She sobbed into her pillow over all the things she'd lost and all the things that could never be.

The next morning, Justine was assisting Dr. Bellamy in dressing a burn on an older woman's leg when Carlita, the receptionist, entered the examining room and informed her that she was wanted on the telephone.

"I'm busy right now, Carlita. If it's one of my sisters—"

She cut in anxiously. "But it's the sheriff, Justine."

Justine could feel patient, doctor and receptionist staring curiously at her. "Perhaps you'd better go answer it, Justine," Dr. Bellamy told her. "I can finish up here."

She gave the older man an appreciative nod. "Thank you. I'll only be a moment or two."

Outside the examining room, Justine hurried down the hallway to the front desk. Carlita had put the receiver back on its hook. She lifted it and punched the glowing line number.

"Hello," she said cooly.

"It's Roy," he replied. "Sorry to bother you at work again, but I didn't want this to wait."

His tone was all business, nothing like the taunting, sexy

way he'd talked to her last night, in the stables. She was relieved.

"You have a lead on the twins?"

"Maybe. There's a man who runs an ice-cream parlor here in Ruidoso who thinks he might have seen them. He says he'd have to see the babies to be sure. Can you bring them into town after work this evening?"

She thought for a moment. "Dr. Bellamy is leaving early this afternoon. I can have the babies in town by four-thirty at the latest. Where do I take them?"

"Meet me at the Ruidoso Police Department. We'll leave from there."

"I don't want to do that," she came back quickly.

For a moment, the line was silent. "What do you mean, you don't want to do it?"

She let out a heavy breath as she glanced down the hallway to the examining rooms. Carlita would be coming back any minute. She didn't want the woman to overhear anything personal she might be saying to Roy.

"I told you last night—I don't want to see you again. Have one of your deputies go with me."

"Are you that afraid of being alone with me?"

"I'm not afraid. I just prefer not to be in your company."

"Well, forget your preferences and be there."

She opened her mouth to tell him no, but he hung up before she could get the word out. Furious, she slammed down the phone just as Carlita arrived at the desk.

"My goodness, you don't look too happy," she said, her dark gaze studying Justine's red cheeks and tight lips.

"Happy? Nothing about Sheriff Pardee makes me happy," she said to the shocked receptionist, then turned and walked quickly back to the examining rooms.

Chapter Four

"Justine, do you really think it's necessary to take the twins into town?" Rose asked later that afternoon, as she helped Justine dress the babies in clean clothes. "It's not likely this man really knows that much. Besides, it would be easier for him to come out here to the ranch than transporting the babies into town."

"I know," Justine agreed. "But apparently that suggestion wasn't put to him. Roy said for me to be there with the babies. And as much as I hate to, I'm going to be there."

In her usual quiet and thoughtful manner, Rose regarded Justine's grim face and flustered movements.

"You don't like Sheriff Pardee much, do you?"

Justine didn't look up from her task as she buttoned a shirt on the boy twin. "Not really."

"Why?"

Justine momentarily closed her eyes, and then her blood began to boil. Before she knew it, words were spilling out of her mouth. "He's just not my type of man. He's arrogant and cocky and he thinks women are playthings. He has no respect for women or families in general. He's callous and hateful and he thinks all he has to do is look at a woman to make her lust after him."

Rose gasped softly. "Justine! My word, where did you come up with such things about a man you barely know? Sheriff Pardee has been kind to us. And when he looked at me, I didn't get the impression he was trying to be suggestive or provocative."

Since Rose rarely had anything good to say about a man, Justine was more than surprised by her sister's outspoken opinion on Roy.

"I just happen to know his kind, Rose. I ought to—I encountered plenty of them in college."

"He doesn't seem like a phony to me," Rose went on.

It was puzzling even to Justine. A few days ago, she'd felt certain any feelings she had toward Roy had died when Charlie was born. But now that he'd kissed her, she knew he'd stirred up a long-buried need inside her.

"That's because you don't know men like I do. But believe me, it doesn't take very long to see through them," Justine said flatly.

Rose frowned as she watched her sister stuff several clean diapers into a duffel bag. "Well, I admit I haven't had as much experience with men as you, but this attitude that you have toward the sheriff seems rather unfair. You make him sound like the cad who ended your engagement and left you pregnant with Charlie."

Justine hoped her face wasn't white as she glanced evasively at her sister. "Believe me, Rose, all men are from the same mold. You ought to know that as well as I."

Rose walked over to the bedroom window and glanced out at the corrals in the distance. Her face was suddenly pinched with pain and disgust. "And you know I'll never forget what Peter did to me, Justine. I'm frigid now because of him."

"Oh, dear heaven, you're not frigid, Rose!" Justine softly scolded her. "You just think you are."

Rose slowly turned back to her sister. "Frigid or not, I realize all men aren't bastards. And I have a feeling that Sheriff Pardee is different from most men out there. I think deep down you know he's different, too."

Justine sighed as she gazed at the two babies lying side by side on the double bed. They were looking up at her with trusting eyes, the same way Charlie did. Her heart surged with love. "Right now, I'm not concerned with Roy. I just want to make sure the twins are taken care of."

A few minutes later, Rose helped her carry the babies and the duffel bag out to her pickup, where the two women had strapped down a double car seat for children.

After securing the babies, Justine climbed behind the steering wheel. "I'll be back as soon as I can. I don't know how long this is going to take. Just make sure Charlie doesn't eat any candy before supper."

Rose nodded and smiled. "He'll be fine. As long as he's with Chloe and the horses, he won't even miss you."

"That really makes me feel needed," Justine said with a grin, then started the engine and pulled the gearshift into drive. "See you later."

Rose stepped back and waved her sister and the twins down the road.

Thirty-five minutes later, Justine pulled into the parking lot in front of Ruidoso's police department. Roy's four-wheel-drive vehicle was parked to one side of the building. She parked beside it and killed the motor.

She didn't know what she was supposed to do now. She wasn't about to leave the twins in the pickup alone while she went inside to find Roy. Nor was she capable of safely carrying both twins into the building with her.

The dilemma was suddenly solved, as Roy and a man who appeared to be one of his deputies walked through the front entrance. The two men paused on the steps and exchanged a few more words before Roy walked over to her vehicle.

"Are you ready to go?" He glanced at the babies, then settled his gaze on Justine's face.

She wanted to stay angry with him, she wanted to look at him and feel nothing, yet she could do neither.

"The babies are strapped in their car seat. Do you want to move it to your vehicle or take mine?" she asked.

He opened the door and motioned for her to scoot over and let him behind the wheel. "It's only a few blocks to the ice-cream parlor," he told her. "This will be faster."

Justine wedged herself as close as she could to the babies, but there just wasn't enough room on the bench seat for her to put space between herself and Roy. His thigh was pressed into hers, and his upper arm pinned her shoulder to the back of the seat. Touching him like this was agony, and she figured he knew it.

"I don't like being manipulated," she said as he steered the pickup onto a main thoroughfare.

He glanced at her. "You think I've done all this just to see you again? What conceit!"

Heat poured into her cheeks. Maybe it had been stupid of her to think he actually *wanted* to see her again. But his behavior last night had warned her to expect anything from him. "Are you saying you didn't want to see me?" she asked, her tone faintly challenging.

"I said I didn't manipulate you."

Justine didn't know what that was supposed to mean, and she wasn't sure she wanted to know. "You could have asked Chloe or Rose to bring the babies into town," she quickly pointed out.

Roy's gaze remained on the traffic. "I don't know Chloe or Rose like I know you."

"Thank God," Justine muttered. "No need for all three Murdock sisters to be corrupted."

"You think that's what I did to you?"

"What you did to me isn't fit for babies' ears," she said.

A frown twisted his profile. "I suppose Charlie's dad treated you better?"

Charlie's dad. Dear God, how she wished she could forget *he* was Charlie's father.

"How he treated me is none of your business," she said flatly, then purposely turned her attention to the twins. The girl had lost her pacifier. She offered it to the baby again, then wiped drool from the boy's chin.

From behind the wheel, Roy was very aware of Justine's soft body pressed against his, the sweet, flowery scent of her, and the way her red hair fell in wild, loose curls down the middle of her back.

Last night, he'd purposely kissed her, to prove to himself that she was totally and irrevocably out of his system. But the kiss hadn't proved anything. Other than the fact that he was still a fool where she was concerned. He still wanted her with a vengeance, and he didn't know what in hell to do about it.

"You sure are testy where Charlie's father is concerned," he said after a moment.

Justine resolutely turned away from the twins and looked him squarely in the face. "Maybe I'm testy where all men are concerned."

His brows lifted at the heat in her voice. "That's not true. You like men."

She gritted her teeth. "You don't know that."

He chuckled under his breath. "I know it better than anybody."

"You only know what you remember," she said tightly. "When I was with you, I was reckless and in-infatuated."

He kept his eyes on the traffic ahead, but Justine could see a muscle working in his jaw. If she'd made him angry, she didn't care. She was just relieved she'd caught herself before she blurted out that she'd been in love with him.

She didn't want Roy to ever know how much she'd cared for him. It was safer to let him think she'd carelessly moved on to some other man.

Roy told himself to forget the woman beside him. She was trouble. That was all she'd ever been in his life. Yet all he could think about was the way she'd tasted last night, the way she'd made love to him all those years ago. She'd given herself to him in a way that no woman had since. She'd branded him deep inside, and now that she was back in the Hondo Valley, he felt like a marked man.

The ice-cream parlor was at the west end of town, where the street began to climb up into the mountains. Along with ice cream, the shop also served sandwiches and short orders. At this time of the evening, the place was beginning to fill up with after-work diners.

After unfastening the babies from the car seat, Roy took the boy and Justine carried the girl. They found a small table in one corner of the room and waited for a waitress. When she finally arrived, Roy glanced at Justine.

"Do you want something to eat?"

She'd thought this was supposed to be strictly a police visit, but he was making it seem like a family outing with the kids, Justine thought with a measure of surprise. And from the curious glances the four of them were receiving from the other diners, she suspected they were equally surprised to see their county sheriff with a woman and a couple of babies.

"No, thank you. I'll eat later, with my sisters."

"What about the babies?"

The twins had taken a bottle an hour or more before Justine headed into town with them. At their age, they would probably be getting hungry before she got the two of them home.

"I suppose we could feed them some vanilla ice cream," she said.

"We?"

She slanted him a dry look. "You can handle a spoon, can't you?"

With a sigh, he glanced up at the hovering waitress. "Vanilla ice cream for the kids, and two coffees. Also, tell Fred that Sheriff Pardee is here. He'll know what I want."

The waitress flashed him a ready smile. "Yes, sir. Can I get anything else for you?"

"No, thanks. That will do it."

The young woman hurried away to do the sheriff's bidding. Justine's lips curved with faint amusement. "I wonder what she would have done if you'd asked for the moon?"

He flashed her an annoyed glance. "You're being nasty."

Justine shrugged innocently. "Not really. She was bedazzled by you."

"She was simply doing her job."

Justine's eyes clashed with his, then drifted down to the hard line of his mouth. She didn't have to recall what it had been like last night to have those lips pressed against hers. The image was already burning through her mind.

"She would have liked to do more."

Would you? The question was in his eyes. But whether he was going to speak it aloud to her, Justine would never know, because the baby boy on his knee grabbed for the saltshaker.

Roy's hand flashed out, took hold of the eager little fist and guided it away from the table.

"No, son," he told the wide-eyed boy. "That stuff isn't good for big people, much less a little tot like you."

The baby seemed to think having Roy talk to him was quite amusing, and he burst out with a happy little shriek.

Roy rubbed his ear in the aftermath. "What a mouth on this kid!"

Justine couldn't help but smile. "He likes you."

Roy glanced from Justine to the baby's dimpled face. "You think he does?"

"Why does that shock you? To hear you tell it, everybody likes you. Ninety percent of the vote. I guess you can include Adam in that ninety percent now."

He glanced sharply at Justine. "Adam? You've named him?"

With a weary shake of her head, Justine said, "I didn't name the twins. My sisters did. Anna for the girl. Adam for the boy."

Justine scooted the wiggling Anna up farther in her lap, while Roy studied her with narrowed eyes.

"I told you, Justine, this is a temporary thing. You can't name these children!"

Justine sighed. "Yes. I know you're right, Roy. But I can hardly control what my sisters do. Besides, we can't simply keep calling them 'baby boy' or 'baby girl.' The two of them ought to at least have temporary names. Until you can come up with their real ones."

Before he could make a reply, the waitress arrived with the coffee and ice cream.

Justine placed her coffee safely out of Anna's reach, then tucked a napkin into the collar of the baby's dress.

Watching her, Roy asked, "Do I need to put one of those on him, too?"

Justine could have reached across the small table and put a makeshift bib on Adam herself, but she wasn't going to. It was obvious that he didn't want to be a father or have to do the things that being a father sometimes required. But that was too bad, she thought smugly. Taking care of Adam for a few minutes would be good for the man.

"Adam would probably appreciate not having ice cream all over his shirt."

Grunting with annoyance, he reached for a napkin. "This is—" He paused as he awkwardly tucked the paper around the baby's throat. "You can't just expect me to pick up a baby and know what to do with him."

The sight of Roy's big hand against Adam's little cheek

stirred a bittersweet ache in Justine. This man was Charlie's father, yet he'd never touched his son. He'd never held him or fed him or kissed his cheek.

Maybe if he'd known about Charlie... Her regretful thoughts skidded to a jarring halt. If Roy had known about Charlie, he would have become a father to him out of obligation. Justine wanted more than that for her son. He deserved more, and so did she.

"It won't hurt you to learn," she said, trying her best to sound casual. "You might want to become a father someday."

He snorted, and Justine's heart cringed.

"I doubt I'll ever become a husband, much less a father," he told her.

Justine's eyes dropped to the crown of Anna's red head. "In other words, you still don't want a family."

If there was a caustic sound to her words, Roy didn't appear to notice. He spooned into the small mound of ice cream, then offered it to Adam. The boy promptly opened his mouth, and Roy cautiously slipped the spoon inside.

"It's not a matter of what I want," Roy said after a moment. "It's just that I—" He paused and gestured toward both twins. "This isn't for me. I'm a sheriff and a rancher. What time I'm not doing law work, I'm taking care of cattle and horses. Besides, I never met a woman I wanted to get that close to."

Other than you, Roy very nearly added, but he stopped himself short of that admission. It was bad enough that Justine had walked away from him without a word. The last thing he wanted was for her to know just how much she'd hurt him. She'd made his life sweet, filled it with purpose and meaning. He'd been able to talk to her about anything and everything. She'd not only been his lover, she'd also been his friend and companion. Since then, Roy had never found another woman who could fill the empty hole she'd left in him.

Deciding she'd heard enough of his cutting remarks, Justine put all her attention into feeding little Anna. After a few moments passed in silence, a burly man with balding gray hair and a thick walrus mustache approached their table.

"Hello, Roy. I see you made it in with the kids," the man said, casting an eye at the twins and Justine.

"Fred, this is Justine Murdock. She's the lady who found the twins," Roy told him.

Fred grinned with recognition. "She's also the lady who gave me a shot the last time I visited Dr. Bellamy."

Justine nodded and smiled. "I hope I didn't hurt you too badly."

Fred laughed and winked. "Best shot I ever had. Didn't feel a thing. 'Course, it makes it a lot easier for a man to get jabbed with a needle when he has a beautiful woman to look at."

Roy made a big production of clearing his throat. "What about the babies, Fred? Do you remember seeing them in here? Or was it another set of twins altogether?"

The middle-aged man stepped back from the table and carefully eyed both Adam and Anna, then nodded. "Yep, I'm pretty sure these are the two who were in here that day. I remember the boy having slightly darker red hair, and the girl had brighter hair like you, Ms. Murdock." His expression suddenly turned thoughtful, as his gaze went from Justine to Anna and back again. "I know this sounds odd, but something about these babies look like you."

Justine's mouth dropped open. "Me? Oh, no. It must be their red hair that's making you think such a thing," she said with faint amusement. "I have one child of my own, but I certainly haven't given birth to twins."

"Well, like I said, I know it sounds crazy, but they both resemble you. Something about the chins, and the tilt of their eyes."

Justine searched the babies' faces as she offered Anna

more ice cream. She hadn't seen a part of herself in either twin, but then, she'd had no reason to look.

Roy spoke up. "I think you're right, Fred. I hadn't noticed until you pointed it out."

Justine glanced from one man to the other. "You're both ridiculous. How could these twins favor me? I don't even know anyone who's had twins, much less anyone who's related to me!"

Ignoring her protest, Roy asked Fred, "Can you describe the person who was with the babies?"

Fred shrugged. "A little. It was a woman. In her thirties, I'd say. She had dark hair that came to somewhere around here." He measured a spot at the base of his neck. "She put the babies in high chairs and left them at the table while she went to the ladies' room."

"How do you remember that? Yesterday you weren't sure you'd even seen the babies," Roy reminded him.

Fred gave his mustache a thoughtful rub. "I just remember, Roy. Now that I've seen the babies, I know it was them. They came in the afternoon, while there was a lull in the place. I came out from the kitchen to fill the saltshakers. That's when I noticed that she got up and went to the ladies' room."

"Did you speak to her at any time? Get her name? Did you notice the vehicle she was driving?"

Fred looked regretful. "Didn't notice what she was driving. I only asked her how she was doing, that's all. I didn't make conversation with her. Some women don't take to that, and besides, she seemed antsy to me."

"What do you mean, antsy?" Roy asked.

Adam had discovered Roy's badge again, and was pulling on it with great concentration. While waiting for Fred to answer, he disengaged the baby's fingers.

"Oh, you know, Roy," the man went on. "Kinda nervous-like. But I didn't think anything about it. I figured it would make most any woman nervous to care for two little ones like this without any help.''

Roy nodded and glanced over at Justine. She was wiping Anna's face, and as he watched her, he didn't have to wonder what kind of mother she was. Charlie had a tender, attentive mother. One who would protect him fiercely and love him with every fiber of her being. But that didn't surprise Roy. He instinctively knew that Justine would be passionate about anyone she loved. She just hadn't loved him that way.

"Don't worry about it, Fred. What I'd like for you to do is get together with a composite artist and see if you can come up with a close likeness of the woman. I'll have to call an artist in from Albuquerque, and that may take a day or two, but when he or she arrives, I'll let you know."

"Sure, Roy. I'll be glad to help."

The two men talked for a minute or two more before Fred left to go back to the kitchen. Once they were alone again, Justine looked at Roy. "What do you think? Do you believe he really remembers the twins and the woman?"

Roy nodded. "I also think he hit the mark when he said Anna and Adam, or whatever their real names are, resemble you."

Justine let out a long, impatient breath. "Roy, I'll say it again. That notion is farfetched."

Shrugging, he took a sip of his coffee. "Maybe so. But I want a list of your relatives."

"You know my relatives."

"I'm talking distant ones now."

Anna began to squirm and fuss. Justine stood the baby up against her shoulder and patted her back. "Well, let's see, we have an elderly uncle on my mother's side. He lives in a nursing home in Texas."

"Does he have children?"

Justine shook her head. "Never married."

"We can mark him off."

Justine tapped the tabletop with her fingertips as she went down a mental list in her mind. "There's an aunt on my mother's side, also. She lives in Colorado. She's married and in her sixties. She could never have children. Then there was a brother of Dad's. He's been dead several years. He had a son and daughter. Both of them are a little older than my sisters and myself."

"Do they have children, or could they perhaps have had twins and decided to dump them on the Bar M?"

It was a preposterous idea, but Justine supposed in this sort of situation Roy needed to cover every angle. "I have no idea where either of my cousins are now. The last we heard, Neil had been in trouble with the law, and Earlene, his sister, was living in some sort of commune up in one of the northern states. The whole family was strange, and never really associated with us."

"Do you have any old addresses? We might be able to trace them. It's a slim chance, but we have to start somewhere."

She nodded. "I'll look for them tonight."

"The woman that Fred just described to us, does she sound familiar? Like one of your relatives?"

Justine quickly shook her head. "The only female cousin I have is Earlene, the one I mentioned to you. She's a large blond woman. Of course, it's not unusual for a woman to change her hair color."

Adam began banging both fists on the tabletop. Roy tucked the baby beneath the crook of his arm, then scooted the both of them back from the table. "Do babies never just sit still?" he asked Justine, while studying the child on his lap. "Looks to me like after a few minutes of this he'd be all tuckered out. I'm already getting that way."

"They're both going to get fussy and tired if I don't get them back home," Justine told him. "Are you ready to go?"

His lips curved mockingly. "Are you that anxious to get rid of my company?"

She was and she wasn't. Being with Roy this evening hadn't been all bad. But it hadn't necessarily been good for her, either. He made her think things, remember things, that were better left gone and forgotten. Still, she couldn't deny that Roy Pardee pulled on her like a magnet. She didn't want to be close to him, but she was drawn to him anyway.

"We've done what we came to do," she said crisply. "I have things to do at home, and I'm sure you have plenty of work to get back to."

He studied her face for so long that Justine shifted on her seat and frowned at him. "What's wrong? Why are you looking at me like that?"

"I'm trying to figure why you think it's necessary to give me an iceberg act."

"I'm not acting."

"What would you rather call it, then? Lying? Because I can see from the color in your cheeks that you're feeling anything but cool."

She took a deep, calming breath. It didn't help. "The color in my cheeks is there because you're annoying me."

He couldn't help saying, "You used to enjoy spending time with me."

For a moment, Justine was knocked off kilter by his words. She hadn't expected him to be thinking back. Especially about her and him. "I used to enjoy a lot of things about you," she said quietly. "But you're not the same you, and I'm not the same me."

Adam's hand was on Roy's, the soft little fingers patting his knuckles, then gripping his forefinger. It surprised Roy, just how precious the baby's touch was to him. And at that moment, with the child on his lap and Justine sitting across the table from him, he wondered exactly what he might have missed by not having a family. A family with her.

"We're the same, only older," he said.

"I hope you're wrong about that, Roy. Neither one of us was very smart when we were...together."

Together. That word sounded so warm and sweet to him. Yet he didn't understand why. Being together with Justine was not what he wanted. She was ice and fire. She would have him crazy before he could turn around once. So why was he so reluctant to leave and send her on her way? Why couldn't he forget and go on to some other woman?

Because he didn't want another woman, he realized with a start. God only knew how hard he'd tried to find another one after Justine left town. In the past years, he'd had several women in his arms and in his bed. Yet none of them had stirred him as much as Justine could with just one look.

"We might not have been smart, but we were happy. For a while."

Justine glanced at him, then tore her eyes away. She didn't want to think of the brief happiness they'd once shared. It hurt too much.

Grabbing her purse, she clutched Anna to her shoulder and rose to her feet. "Well, you know how the old saying goes—ignorance is bliss."

The cynical tone of her voice jerked Roy out of his melancholy thoughts. Tightening his hold on Adam, he dug his wallet out of his jeans, then tossed a few bills down on the tabletop.

"Yeah, well, as far as I know, I'm neither ignorant or blissful. So I guess I have changed."

Justine felt too miserable to say anything else. Roy got to his feet and caught hold of her elbow.

"Let's get out of here," he muttered. "I think we've enjoyed about as much of each other as we can stand for one day."

A few minutes later, as Justine drove the twins back to the Bar M, she couldn't shake Roy from her mind. The more she saw of him, the more she was beginning to realize he wasn't quite the unfeeling, steely-eyed sheriff she'd first believed. This evening, she'd seen flashes of tenderness in him when he dealt with Adam, and later, when he spoke of the two of them once being happy together, Justine had been certain she heard regret in his voice.

But then his mood had turned dark. She knew she could blame herself for that. She'd goaded him with her flip remarks. As far as that went, she could blame herself for a part of their breakup. Yet that wouldn't do any good. It was over between them. When was she finally going to realize that?

That night, as she sat on the floor in her father's office, searching for her cousins' addresses, Chloe came into the room, carrying a fresh cup of steaming coffee.

"Knock, knock," she called.

Justine smiled at her younger sister. "I hope that coffee is for me."

"It is. I thought you might need a break."

Justine took the cup and saucer from her, took a sip, then motioned to the pile of old papers and envelopes on the floor beside her. "Still no luck. I'm afraid I'm going to have to tell Roy I can't find our cousins' addresses."

"Did you try looking through Mother's bag of old Christmas cards? You know she rarely ever threw correspondence away."

Justine's face brightened. "Good idea. I'll look in a minute. But right now," she said with a contented sigh, "I'm going to drink this."

While Justine sipped the coffee, Chloe plopped down in a desk chair and crossed her legs.

"How are things going with the horses?" Justine asked her. "I've been so busy these past few days, I haven't asked you how your work with the yearlings is coming along."

"Slowly. But I can already tell the Pie in the Sky filly is going to have rockets on her feet. She loves to run."

Justine couldn't help but smile at the faint excitement in Chloe's voice. At least the ranch's financial problems hadn't taken away her hope for the future. "That's good to hear. Maybe she'll win us a million in the All-American Futurity."

Chloe chuckled. "Yeah, wouldn't that be something? Daddy would be bursting with pride. If he were here," she added, her face suddenly shadowed with loss.

"Daddy would want you to go on with training the horses, whether he was here to see it or not," Justine said gently.

Her eyes on the floor, Chloe nodded, then brought her gaze back up to Justine. "I know you're right," she said, and then her eyes slowly scanned Justine's tired features. "Aunt Kitty said you came home in a snit this evening."

Justine's mouth fell open. She thought she'd been behaving in a perfectly normal manner since her trip into town. But apparently her family knew her better than she thought. "I wasn't in a snit. Where did she get that idea?"

Chloe shrugged. "She said you were nearly in tears."

Justine grimaced. "Aunt Kitty exaggerates. There was nothing wrong with me, except exhaustion."

The toe of Chloe's cowboy boot tapped the air. "She thinks there's something about the sheriff and you—"

Justine's head whipped up. "There's nothing between Roy and me! What makes her think that?"

Chloe smiled to herself. "Maybe it's the way you say his name.... Roy. It comes out sounding more than friendly."

"What imaginations you two have," Justine muttered. "Roy is only an old acquaintance who happens to rub me the wrong way. That's all!"

Justine's protests were a bit too loud to satisfy Chloe, but the younger Murdock sister decided to let the whole matter slide for the moment. "So what do you think about this woman who was supposedly with the twins? Think it was their mother?''

Justine shrugged. ''Who's to say?''

Chloe remained silent for so long, Justine finally glanced at her. ''Chloe? Is something wrong?''

The younger woman sighed. ''I don't want Sheriff Pardee to find the twins' parents.''

''Chloe! That's terrible. You should be thinking about the babies and their welfare.''

''I am,'' she shot back. ''I don't want them taken away from us and given back to parents who are—well, obviously unfit to be parents!''

''Chloe, we don't know any circumstances yet. Roy might discover that the twins have been kidnapped from a loving family.''

''No!'' she said with a violent shake of her head. ''I know in my heart that the babies were meant to be here with us.''

Justine didn't argue any further. She could see that Chloe had already set her heart on keeping the babies, and who was she to dash her hopes?

Lola Murdock's old Christmas cards proved to be fruitful. Justine wrote down a Nebraska address for Neil. She couldn't find an address for Earlene, but she did discover a short letter folded inside one card that said Earlene was living in Idaho, somewhere north of Boise.

Maybe the information would be enough for Roy to start on, she thought. But in her opinion, her two weird cousins had nothing to do with Adam and Anna.

Glancing at her watch, she decided it was too late to call Roy tonight. Tomorrow was Saturday. As much as she hated to talk with him again, she'd call his home in the morning. The quicker he could solve this mystery of the babies, the quicker he would be out of her life for good. And that was what she wanted, she told herself fiercely.

She didn't want to have to see him, touch him, hear his voice or remember how much she'd once loved him.

She'd been devastated when she lost Roy, and afraid to have his baby alone. But she'd lived through it all, and survived. Only now...now she was beginning to think she still loved him, and the idea terrified her.

Chapter Five

Justine didn't have to call Roy the next morning. She was finishing the last of her coffee at the kitchen table with Kitty when the telephone rang.

She went to answer it, and was faintly surprised when she heard Roy's voice on the other end of the line.

"Do you have news about the twins?" she asked, before he could say anything.

"No. I'm not calling about the twins," he said.

Her heart began to thud with heavy dread. She glanced at Kitty and saw the woman watching her curiously. "Then what is it?"

He suddenly chuckled, and the sound shivered over her. "Still playing it cool, are you?"

"My cheeks aren't red," she countered, doing her best to keep her voice low. "Now what do you want?"

"Actually, I'm calling about Charlie," he said.

His laughter had caught her off guard, but this really stunned her. "Charlie? My son?"

He frowned at the panic in her voice. "Why, yes. Why? Is something wrong with him?"

Placing her hand over the mouthpiece, she drew in a long breath, let it out, then drew in another. "No. There's nothing wrong with him. He's watching cartoons. But I don't understand why—"

"He talked to me the other day about his horse. Thundercloud, I believe he called him."

Justine relaxed slightly. "Yes. He's crazy about the animal."

"I gathered that. So I thought you might drive him over here to the ranch. I have something I think he'd enjoy seeing."

Justine couldn't believe he was inviting her and Charlie to his home. She'd only been there once, and that had been years ago. "I don't know if that would be wise," she started.

"Hellfire, Justine! I'm not inviting you over here to seduce you!"

Her spine went rigid. "I didn't think you were! But Charlie doesn't know you, and—"

"Yes, he does. He knows I'm the sheriff, and he thinks I'm the boss."

Justine closed her eyes against her spinning thoughts. "And you like it when anyone thinks of you as the boss," she said dryly.

He chuckled under his breath. "I'd like it if you did."

Dear heaven, he was a flirt, she thought with a groan. Six years hadn't taken that out of him. "To be truthful, I was just about to call you myself. I found an address for my cousin."

"Good. Bring it when you come."

"Roy—"

The line went dead, and she knew he'd hung up so that she wouldn't have a chance to say no.

Jamming the phone back on its hook, she swiped a frustrated hand through her tangled hair. What was she going to do now?

"Justine? Was that Sheriff Pardee?"

Justine glanced absently across the room at her aunt. "I'm afraid so."

"What did he want? Does he have a new lead on the case?"

Justine wanted to scream. "No. Is Charlie still in his pyjamas?"

Kitty frowned. "I don't know. Why?"

"Because the sheriff wants to see him," she said sharply.

Her face full of concern, Kitty rose from the table and walked over to where Justine still stood, by the telephone. "Okay, honey, I want to know what's going on. And I'm not simply being a nosy old aunt. I can see you're troubled. You look troubled every time you say the sheriff's name."

With her hand on her forehead, Justine tilted her face toward the ceiling. "What is it with you and my sisters? You all seem to think I have this thing for Roy, when—"

"Don't give me that cock-and-bull runaround. This is your old wizened aunt who's been down the road and seen a mile or two. I realize that you and the sheriff have had to meet because of the twins. But that doesn't account for the way the two of you look at each other."

"Aunt Kitty—"

"Now, don't interrupt when I've got my fires burning. I'm not blind or deaf. I can see that Roy is more to you than just an old acquaintance or high school classmate. You were lovers, weren't you?"

To Justine's surprise, it was a relief that her aunt had finally guessed the truth. Roy had been in her heart for so long, but there had been no one, not her parents, not her sisters, not anyone, that she could say his name to and cry. That she could tell how much she'd loved him and how much it had hurt her to let him go.

Before she realized it, tears were streaming down her cheeks and her aunt was holding her tightly in her arms.

"My dear honey girl," she said, patting Justine's trembling shoulder. "What a burden you've been carrying around inside you."

"Oh, Aunt Kitty, I thought when Mother got sick that I could come back home and never have to see him again. And I didn't see him until the twins showed up and I had to call him. I thought then that facing him again wouldn't hurt. But it did. It still does."

Kitty gently put Justine away from her and looked directly into her teary green eyes. "Roy is Charlie's father, isn't he?"

Justine's throat was so clogged she could merely nod.

"I thought as much. The other night, I noticed the boy favors him in ways. His walk and gestures. His blue eyes and sandy hair. Does Roy know?"

Justine shook her head. "No. And he never will."

"Why?"

Groaning, Justine turned away from her aunt and desperately wiped at her eyes. "Because— There's lots of reasons."

Kitty's lips pressed together in a thin line. "Roy doesn't love you? Is that the reason?"

"Roy never loved anyone but himself. But I'm not keeping Charlie from his father simply because he doesn't love me. I'm not that selfish." She glanced over her shoulder at Kitty. "When Roy and I— When Charlie was conceived, Roy wasn't ready for a family, and I didn't want to trap him that way."

"And what about now?" Kitty asked, her expression full of concern. "Six years have passed, Roy might feel differently after all this time."

Justine shook her head. "No. He told me himself, just yesterday, that he wasn't cut out to be a father or a family man."

Kitty snorted. "Most all men say that. They have to say it, because they don't want to admit they're afraid of becoming husbands and daddies. Why, even your father was gun-shy before your mother roped him in.''

"Roy is different."

Kitty dismissed Justine's idea with a wave of her hand. "Roy is a man. And he looks at you with enough heat to set a house on fire. Why don't you do something about it?''

"Because I don't want to do anything about it. Because Roy hurt me once, and I won't allow him to do it twice.'' Desperate to escape the hemmed-in feeling coming over her, Justine skirted around her aunt and walked over to the open screen door leading out to the back courtyard. After a moment, she sighed, then said, "If Roy wants anything from me, and that's a big *if,* the anything would be sex, pure and simple.''

From behind her, Kitty laughed. "Oh, Justine, there's many a woman who would give anything to have Roy Pardee attracted to them in that way. He's strong, intelligent, good-looking, and too sexy for any woman to resist.''

The idea of Roy with just *any* woman was sickening to Justine. Though it shouldn't have been. If he was involved with another woman, she could breathe a sigh of relief. Yet she couldn't stand the idea of him marrying someone, making love to her, giving her a child. Justine supposed that because she'd loved him so much and borne his son, she'd somehow always thought of him as her man. Which was crazy. Roy wasn't her man, and never had been.

"I guess I'm just not like other women, Aunt Kitty. I want more than that, and Roy can't give it to me.''

Kitty let out a hopeless sigh. Then, walking up behind her, she placed a hand on Justine's arm. "I would like to know something, Justine.''

"What?''

"Why you kept Charlie's parentage a secret. Why did you not tell your parents, your sisters? Instead, you let us all believe you were engaged to a college student and he was the one who'd left you pregnant.''

A pang of regret lanced through her chest. "Because I—I was ashamed of myself for getting involved with a man who was a—a philanderer. I didn't want them to think badly of me. But more than that, I didn't want anyone, especially Roy, putting two and two together and wondering if Charlie was his son. And, oddly enough, I didn't want to ruin his reputation."

Kitty stared thoughtfully at her niece's bent head. "Why in the world would you be worried about his reputation? You should have wanted to smear him in the dirt."

Justine let out a deep sigh. "Roy was a deputy then, everyone liked and respected him. And when I realized things weren't going to work for us, I was devastated, I hated him, or I thought I did, and told myself I could never forgive him. But I didn't want to humiliate him by dragging his name through the mud. I guess I still don't. Crazy, huh?"

"Love is crazy, Justine. And I think you need to face the fact that you still love Roy Pardee."

An hour and a half later, Justine turned her pickup down a dusty side road and through an arched-pipe entrance with a sign announcing that she was on the Pardee Ranch.

On the bench seat beside her, Charlie stared curiously out the windshield. "Is this the way to Sheriff Roy's house?"

"Yes. It will only be a few minutes until we get there now."

He looked at his mother. "Why are we going there, Mommy? Does he think we've done something bad?"

Justine smiled at him. "No, darling. I've got to give Roy a paper, and he—wanted you to come along, too."

Charlie's face brightened. "Do you think Sheriff Roy likes me?"

Justine had never been an overly emotional woman, yet

she suddenly felt tears clogging her throat. "I'm sure he does. You're a pretty easy boy to like."

Charlie giggled, but then his little face sobered. "Well, I couldn't tell if Sheriff Roy liked me, 'cause he don't smile very much. Why doesn't he smile, Mommy? Is he a sad man?"

Justine darted a glance at her son as she went over the question in her mind. Was Roy a sad man, or had he simply grown hard?

"I don't know, Charlie. A sheriff is a very busy guy. He has to protect a lot of people. It might be that he forgets to smile."

Charlie tilted his head one way and then the other as he contemplated his mother's words. "Then we'd better remind him."

If only it could be that simple, Justine thought.

The distance from the Bar M to the Pardee Ranch was not that far, but in those few miles the landscape began to change. The mountains began to slope off into desert hills covered with sage, scrubby creosote, piñon pine and choya cactus. The area was a startling change from the heavily forested mountains in Ruidoso, but it was equally beautiful to Justine.

Roy's home was a split-log structure built near the edge of the Hondo River. A row of poplars and several cottonwood trees shaded the house and the yard. There was hardly any grass to speak of, and the closest thing to a flower was a blooming prickly pear growing at the edge of the barbed-wire fence.

Justine parked the pickup near the front of the house. By the time she and Charlie had climbed to the ground, a collie was there to greet them with a friendly bark.

"Don't worry. He doesn't bite."

She looked up to see Roy rounding the corner of the house. This morning he was dressed in jeans and boots and a plain blue work shirt. The absence of his badge and gun made him seem more approachable, somehow, and more like the man she'd first fallen in love with.

To her disgust, she felt a faint smile tugging at her lips. "Hello," she said.

He came to stand a few steps away from them, his eyes running slowly over Justine, then on to Charlie, who was on his knees, hugging the collie around the neck.

"Hello," he replied. "I'm glad you decided to come."

"You really didn't give me much choice, did you?"

A little grin crooked his lips, and suddenly, deep in her heart, Justine could admit to herself just how happy it made her to see him.

"Oh, I think you could have come up with some excuse if you'd wanted to."

"I'm not a woman who would ever stand in the way of the law," she said lightly, then pulled a small slip of paper from the back pocket of her blue jeans and handed it to him.

Roy read it, then nodded. "You couldn't find anything on the female? Her name was Earlene, wasn't it?"

"I couldn't find an address for her, but I did find a short letter from her mother saying she was living in a small town north of Boise, Idaho. That was three years ago."

"Old information is better than none at all," he said. Then, turning away from Justine, he squatted down on his heels in front of Charlie and the dog.

"What do you think about Levi?"

Charlie gave him a broad grin. "He's got sandburs in his hair, but he's pretty. Does he help you round up the cows?"

Roy was impressed. He hadn't expected the boy to know about working dogs or rounding up cows. "He sure does. He can do more work than two cowboys put together."

Forgetting the dog for a moment, Charlie inspected Roy with the bold innocence of a child. "You're not wearing your gun or badge,'' he said. ''Who's gonna be the sheriff today?''

''I'm still the sheriff. But I'm taking today off. Unless something really bad happens, my deputies will take care of things.''

Smiling happily, Charlie continued to pat the dog's head. ''That's good. Because Mommy says you work too hard.''

Roy cut his eyes up to Justine. ''So your mother thinks I work too hard, does she?''

Justine could feel heat splotching her cheeks. Charlie had embarrassed her before, by repeating things he shouldn't. All children did that to their parents. But she'd rather it happen with anyone other than Roy.

''Yep,'' Charlie answered. ''She say that's why you don't smile. I thought you were just sad. But Mommy says you get so busy being the sheriff you forget to smile.''

''Well, I guess I do forget sometimes,'' he told Charlie. Then, rising to his full height, he looked at Justine, his brows arched with a dry presumptuousness. ''I didn't realize you were concerned about my emotional health.''

''I'm not. Charlie is.''

His eyes searched hers, as though he were trying to find something more revealing than her words. Justine nervously folded her hands in front of her and glanced away at the desert hills.

After a moment, Roy gave up and turned to Charlie. ''Come along, son,'' he said, taking the child by the hand. ''I have something down at the barn I want you to see.''

''Can Mommy come, too?'' Charlie asked him.

''Of course. If she wants to,'' he added with a glance at Justine.

Without a word, she fell into step behind the two of them. As they walked behind the house and toward the corrals in the distance, she was acutely aware that Charlie was with his father and Roy was with his son. Yet neither of them knew.

Guilt crushed down on her like the sudden blow of a sledgehammer. What was she doing? Why was she not allowing Charlie to have a father? His real father? And why was she keeping Charlie from Roy? Was she being a selfish, vindictive woman?

No, she thought miserably. She was keeping her secret because Roy didn't want a family. He'd told her so only yesterday. She wasn't about to force a ready-made one on him. He'd only resent her for burdening him with such a responsibility. And who was to say that he would even want to be a real father to Charlie? she asked herself. Not having a father would be better for Charlie than having one that didn't want him.

At the barn, Roy opened a big double door that allowed them to walk through the structure and out to the back, where another maze of corrals was constructed of metal pipe. Inside one of the pens was a painted mare, saddled and tied to the railing. Next to her, in a connecting pen, was a spotted colt.

The moment Charlie saw the two horses, he pointed with excitement.

"Look, Mommy! Look at the colt! It looks like Thundercloud!"

"I believe he's a bit smaller," Justine told her son. "He's not big enough to ride yet."

"Sugar Boy was a yearling in March," Roy told them. "And that's his mother, Brown Sugar."

Charlie's blue eyes glowed at the sight of the painted quarter horses. "Can I go pet them?" he asked Roy.

"Sure. But be careful of Sugar Boy. He likes to take a nibble now and then."

"I'll swat his nose!" Charlie promised, already in a run to the horses.

Roy and Justine followed at a slower pace. The sky was cloudless, and the sun was warm without being too hot. The day couldn't have been more beautiful, but Justine was afraid to relax and enjoy it. Minute by minute, she was seeing Roy in a different light, and she was afraid that if she spent much more time with him, she'd break down and tell him something he wouldn't want to hear. Like how she'd never gotten over him.

"I thought you didn't like children," she said as they ambled across the dusty pen.

"Where did you get that idea?"

She shrugged. "Just an impression."

"I've never had the opportunity to be around children much, except for the juveniles and runaways that come through the sheriff's department. They're not exactly good examples to learn by."

"No. I don't expect so."

Roy watched Charlie gently stroking the mare's nose. "It's refreshing to see a little boy like Charlie who hasn't yet been corrupted by his peers or ruined by a dysfunctional family."

Justine figured that, more often than not, Roy did see the bad side of children. The bad side of humankind in general. She didn't know how he dealt with it, day in and day out. Especially when he had no one close to share it all with.

"To be honest, I was surprised that you asked me to bring him over this morning. The first evening you came out to investigate the twins, I got the feeling Charlie made you uncomfortable."

He stopped a short distance from Charlie and propped his arms on the top railing of the corral. Justine stood a small step away, watching a pensive look settle over his face as he turned his profile toward the distant hills.

"It wasn't Charlie himself that bothered me. It was—"

Justine waited for him to finish. When he didn't, she moved closer and touched his arm.

"It was what?" she asked.

He turned his head slightly toward her. His eyes were shaded by the brim of his hat, but Justine could see that they were clouded. With anger? Pain? Loss? She didn't quite know.

"I couldn't believe you'd given birth to another man's child," he said. Then, with a self-deprecating snort, he gave her a little mocking smile. "Charlie should have been mine. Instead, you ran off and gave yourself to some other man."

She opened her mouth as questions begged to be released, but she couldn't voice any of them. For the first time since she'd come home to the Hondo Valley, she was afraid she'd made a mistake in keeping her pregnancy from Roy six years ago. And she was even more afraid she was going to make a bigger one now.

"Roy, I wish—"

Before she could finish, Charlie raced over to them, his face lit with excitement.

"Do you have any more horses, Roy?"

"I have two more in the barn," he told the boy. "If your mother wants to, I'll saddle them, and we can all go for a ride. You can have Brown Sugar for a mount. How would that be?"

Charlie's eyes grew wider and wider as he looked from the painted mare to Roy, and then on to his mother.

"Do you want to, Mommy? Can we go for a ride with Sheriff Roy?"

She'd never seen her son so animated, and she knew she could hardly tell him no. It would be cruel and selfish of her not to allow Charlie to enjoy such a simple thing as a horseback ride.

"If Roy really wants to go to the trouble of saddling the horses, then I guess we could ride for a while."

"Oh, boy!" Charlie cried, then flung his arms around his mother's legs and hugged her tightly. "Thank you, Mommy!"

She rubbed the top of his head. "I believe you should be thanking Sheriff Roy. He's the one who invited you."

Without a moment's hesitation, Charlie ran to Roy and

gave him the same bear hug he'd bestowed on his mother.
For a moment Roy was taken aback by the display of affection.

"Thank you, Sheriff Roy. I'll ride Brown Sugar real good."

"I know you will, son," Roy told him. Then, bending down, he lifted Charlie and carried him over to the waiting mare.

Once the child was firmly seated in the saddle, Roy adjusted the stirrups to the shortest length possible and gave Charlie the reins. "She's real easy on the mouth. And you don't have to kick her. Just give her a soft little nudge. She'll go where you tell her to go."

Nodding to show that he understood, Charlie reined the mare away, and Brown Sugar began to walk quietly around the small pen. Justine walked over to where Roy stood watching the boy and horse.

"Charlie is a good rider. But not on something spirited. I hope she's gentle enough for him."

"I may not know anything about little boys, but I know my horses. Brown Sugar is as gentle as a lamb. There's no need for you to worry."

Deciding she could trust his judgment, she followed Roy into the barn, yet stood close enough to the open door that she could keep an eye on Charlie.

At the other end of the barn, Roy took two geldings, a bay and a buckskin out of separate stalls, then led them to where Justine was standing in the alleyway.

Handing her the reins, he said, "I'll get the tack and saddles."

Since the horses were unfamiliar to her, Justine kept a firm hold on the bridle reins while Roy stepped into a small room built into one corner of the barn.

After a few moments, he came out carrying a saddle and several blankets.

"Which of these horses is going to be my mount?" she asked as he started to brush down the buckskin.

"This one. He has a better disposition."

Justine noticed he worked quickly, his hands firm but easy as he smoothed blankets across the buckskin's back.

"You know, I didn't realize you were still working your father's ranch," she said after a moment. "I figured being the sheriff was more than enough job for you. Wouldn't it be easier to sell this place and move into Ruidoso?"

"It probably would be easier," he said as he folded the stirrup onto the saddle seat, then lifted it onto the horse. "But this is my home. It has been since the day I was born. I don't want to live anywhere else, and I like raising cattle, even though they aren't worth much on the market right now. Besides, I may not be reelected when my term as sheriff is over."

Smiling wryly, she shook her head. "Who are you trying to kid? You'll be the sheriff of Lincoln County as long as you want to be."

"Maybe so," he agreed. "But ranching is in my blood. The same way I suspect it's in yours."

She reached out and stroked the buckskin's neck. "Chloe and Rose are the real ranch women. Both of them can outride me, and they both know infinitely more about cattle than I do. But I like it just the same, and help out wherever I can. Actually, I didn't realize how much I really missed the ranch until I lived away from it," she admitted.

"You were gone a long time."

So very long, she thought. Away from him. Away from her family. She'd felt so lonely. But she'd done her best to hide it, and convince her sisters and parents that she enjoyed living in Las Cruces.

"Yes."

"Why didn't you come home after you graduated? You always told me your intentions were to live here, close to your family."

Keeping her eyes fixed on the horse's dark yellow hair, she said, "Nursing jobs were plentiful there. I wanted to get some experience before I came back to work for a local hospital or doctor."

"You like nursing?"

His question sounded sincere, and Justine wondered if he'd ever wondered about her during the time she was living in Las Cruces. Had he thought of her and the days they'd spent talking and laughing and loving each other? Had he wished that Marla's deception had never torn them apart?

Desperately trying to shake the questions out of her mind, she answered, "I like helping people. Especially those who can't help themselves."

Roy pulled the front saddle cinch tight against the horse and buckled it down. "Well, Marble is ready. If you like, you can lead him outside and hitch him to the fence," he told her.

Glad that Roy had changed the conversation to something less personal, Justine took a moment to study the horse. "Marble?" she asked. "Why in the world do you call him Marble? He doesn't have any spots or dapples. Why not just call him plain old Buck?"

Grinning, Roy took the horse by the nose and turned his face square around to Justine. "Because he has one brown eye, and one white one that looks like a marble."

"Is he blind in the white eye?"

"Not a bit," he assured her. To prove it, Roy made a movement with his hand near the horse's eye, and the animal instinctively blinked.

"Marble," she repeated with a wry grin. "I'd hate to think what sort of name you'd give me. Red, Carrot, Freckles…"

Without warning, he stepped forward and took her chin between his thumb and forefinger. Justine told herself to remain calm. There wasn't any reason for her heart to hammer out of control. He wasn't going to kiss her. Or was he?

"I don't see any freckles," he said, his eyes gliding over her satin-smooth complexion. "You used to have a few on your nose. But I guess you've outgrown them."

So he remembered that about her. What else did he remember, she wondered, as heat seeped into her cheeks, then flared through the rest of her body. "No. They're still there. I cover them up with makeup."

"You shouldn't hide them. They add charm to your face."

His eyes weren't on her freckled nose now, they were on her lips, and Justine was finding it very hard to breathe.

"Sure," she said with wry disbelief. "They're just as charming as the little chip in my tooth and the scar on my forehead."

Roy lifted wispy bangs from her forehead and ran his finger over the faint, crescent-shaped white scar near her hairline. "You were fighting your sister Chloe over a dress, and she hit you with a wooden trinket box," he murmured.

Because he still remembered, her heart contracted painfully. "Roy, why did you ask me to come over this morning? I know you said you wanted to show Charlie the horses, but—"

"You think I asked you over here for other reasons." His mouth twisted cynically as his fingers tightened on her chin. "Do you think I've been pining all these years for you? Do you think I've been counting the days, waiting and hoping that you'd come back to the Hondo Valley—without a husband?"

She didn't like this dark side of him. Maybe because it mirrored the same feelings she'd tried for years to shed, the way a snake sheds its skin. Bitterness, cynicism, blame. They were ugly, painful emotions. She realized that now more than ever.

She swallowed as her eyes fell to the toe of his black boots. "I don't figure you thought of me much at all, Roy."

She actually believed what she was saying, Roy thought incredulously. He could hear it in the depths of her voice. She really did assume that once she'd gone from his sight, she'd gone from his mind. Dear God, if only that were true, he would have been cured of her long ago.

"You never did truly know me, did you?" he asked, his voice low and accusing.

Her eyes clouded with remembered pain. "I thought I did. I even believed you cared for me. I was a fool. I should have known I couldn't trust you."

His blue eyes hardened to steel. "Marla was nothing to me."

Her eyes were equally hard as she held his gaze. "Neither was I."

His nostrils flared. "Is that what you think?"

"It's what I know."

Roy had never meant to get into this with Justine. But one word had led to another, and now he was boiling at her unfair assumptions. "You don't know anything."

"Let me go," she told him through gritted teeth. "I've got to check on Charlie."

"Charlie is fine. I can see him from here. So there's no need to use him for an excuse to get away from me."

She twisted her chin away from his grasp. "I don't have to have an excuse to get away from you!"

Before she could step past him, he grabbed her by both shoulders. "I didn't ask you over here for this, but by heaven, you're going to get it anyway," he growled.

Justine quickly brought her hands up to ward him off. Marble's reins slipped from her grasp, but the horse didn't seem to notice or care. He stood obediently by his master, but Justine was quite another matter. She whacked her fist against the middle of his chest.

"Don't you kiss me! Don't you dare!"

His mouth spread into a sneering smile. "What are you afraid of? Afraid you might like it?"

A short, caustic laugh rolled past her lips. "Don't kid yourself. You could never make me like it!"

The smile on his face deepened, and his eyes were suddenly lit with inner fire. "I take that as a challenge, Justine."

"Roy—"

Her voice faltered as his lips hovered over hers. "No woman has ever said my name like you. Say it again."

He should be asking, not commanding. And she should be telling him to go to hell. But she couldn't. Because, incredibly, somewhere in the growl of his voice, she heard a need in him.

"Roy," she whispered.

As soon as the word was out, his mouth crushed hers. Justine's earlier bravado instantly dissolved into flames as the hungry pressure of his mouth melted all her resistance. With a little moan, she leaned into him and wound her arms around his lean waist.

Roy's arms slipped around her and drew her closer to him. His fingers tangled in the russet-colored tresses lying against her back.

In only a matter of moments, raw desire was surging through him, begging him to forget the pain and humiliation she'd caused him six years ago. His body wanted to make love to her, even though his mind kept telling him he was a crazy fool.

In the end, it was Justine who ended the war being waged inside him. She jerked out of his embrace and turned her back on him.

"You just had to do that, didn't you?"

Her voice was shaky, and her shoulders were visibly trembling. A few moments ago, when she goaded him into kissing her, he'd wanted to show her, prove to her, that he could make her feel, make her hurt for him the same way he'd hurt for her after she went away.

But now he didn't feel a bit proud of himself. He just felt an empty, hollow ache deep in his heart.

"I'm sorry, Justine."

Strangely enough, Justine didn't want an apology from him. She wasn't sure what she wanted from him. "Sorry for what?"

"Sorry that I kissed you. That you didn't like it. That I liked it too much." He scuffed the ground with the toe of his boot. "Hell, I don't know anymore, Justine. I just know, for some reason you make me act crazy."

Sighing, she wiped her tangled hair away from her cheeks and turned to face him. "You said you didn't invite me over here to seduce me," she said. "If that's true, then why did you invite me and my son?"

Justine had always been a frank woman. In the past, she'd never hesitated to speak her mind, whether he approved or not. But now her blunt question caught him off guard.

"I—" His face full of frustration, he shook his head. "I told you, I wanted to show Charlie the horses. Does there have to be another reason, Justine?"

She grimaced. "I've never known you to entertain a child."

Frowning, he snatched up Marble's reins. "Whether you believe it or not, I like your son. He's the first child I've ever really felt drawn to. Maybe that's because you and I were once close. Or maybe it's simply because he's an endearing little boy. Take your pick as to why. But don't read too much into this little outing today. I'm not interested in getting involved with any woman. Even you."

Even if Justine had known what to say to him, she wouldn't have had the chance to open her mouth. Roy turned abruptly and led Marble out of the barn.

She stared after him, his words rolling through her mind.

He's the first child I've ever really felt drawn to. Could it be that Roy instinctively felt a connection with Charlie because they were actually father and son? she wondered. If so, how long would it be before he began to see all the things in Charlie that mirrored him? How long would it be before he discovered the truth—and hated her for it?

Chapter Six

If Justine had any sense at all, she would go pluck Charlie off Brown Sugar, march him and herself to the truck and hightail it back to the Bar M. She and Charlie had survived for five years without Roy. They didn't need him now. And he obviously didn't need anybody but himself.

Her face set with determination, she tied the bay to a nearby post and headed out of the barn. Where Roy was concerned, she'd been stupid six years ago. But she was smarter now, she told herself.

Her stride long and purposeful, she walked out of the dimly lit interior of the barn into the sunny corral. Then her steps faltered. Across the pen, Roy was standing beside the painted mare, his hand resting fondly on the toe of Charlie's boot as he looked up at her son. Their son.

Charlie was grinning from ear to ear, and the happiness on her child's face suddenly wiped away her resolution to leave. Maybe Roy did bring out the worst in her, but he obviously made Charlie happy. And knowing that, she couldn't selfishly deny him time with his father. Especially when Charlie needed a male influence in his life. He missed his grandfather.

"Hi, Mommy!" Charlie called to her, and waved.

She smiled and waved back at him, then walked over to the two of them. "You look like you're having a good time," she said to her son.

"I am! Brown Sugar is really great! She does everything I tell her to. And she doesn't keep walking when I say, 'Whoa.' See how still she's standing?"

Justine nodded, then turned her eyes to Roy. She supposed she should be feeling uncomfortable to face him, after the passionate way she'd returned his kiss in the barn and the heated exchange they'd shared afterward. But she wasn't. Too much had already passed between them for her to be embarrassed.

"Yes, I see," she answered Charlie's question. "Roy must have trained her well."

"He sure did!" Charlie agreed. "She's not a bit spoiled, like Thundercloud!"

Her eyes still on Roy, she said, "Roy doesn't believe in spoiling anything, so that means you better mind him when he tells you to do something."

"I will," Charlie promised.

He nudged Brown Sugar's side, and the horse and boy moved away from the two adults. Once he was out of earshot, Roy turned to Justine. "Why did you say I don't believe in spoiling? You couldn't have known that about me. Or were you just trying to make Charlie believe I'm mean and crotchety?"

Her brows arched as she studied his face. "You don't spoil people or animals, do you?"

He grimaced. "No. But—"

"Then why does it bother you to hear it spoken aloud?"

"I'm not a hard man, Justine."

Her soft laugh was full of disbelief. "Who are you trying

to fool, Roy Pardee? You haven't got a soft spot in your body. You're hard through and through.''

"Is there something wrong with that?"

Shrugging, she turned her eyes on Charlie as he walked the horse slowly around the edge of the corral. "If you're happy, then I guess there isn't a thing wrong with it." She glanced back at him. "Are you going to saddle the bay so we can get started?"

"You're still going riding?"

The surprise on his face curved her lips into an amused smile. "You didn't think one little kiss from you would send me running back home, did you?"

This was the Justine he used to know, Roy thought. The sassy redhead who could turn him inside out with just one look. This Justine was far more dangerous to him than the ice goddess she'd tried to be these past few times he was in her company.

"I never know about you, Justine."

She slanted him a wry, daring look. "Good. I don't want you to know about me," she said. Then, with a shrug, she added, "Besides, this little outing doesn't mean anything. You told me so yourself."

She was goading him, and maybe that should make him angry. But Roy had never liked cowering, submissive women. He supposed that was why Justine's fire had always appealed to him.

"I'll go saddle the bay," he muttered.

She smiled at him. "We'll be waiting."

A few minutes later, Roy guided the three of them south of the house, across the river and into the hills. The horses followed a well-worn cattle trail that wound through the sage and cactus and piñon. Choya was beginning to bloom, deep pink, yellow and red, and now and then a prickly pear offered its roses for view.

The beauty of the land quickly relaxed Justine, and she gazed around the Pardee spread with keen interest. At first glance, it appeared to be barren of grass, but on closer inspection she could see patches of it hidden between the tufts of sagebrush. Even though the grass was sparse, she, like anyone who raised cattle or horses in New Mexico, knew it possessed a high amount of protein.

The three of them had ridden a little more than a mile when Justine spotted a herd of cattle in the distance. The mixed breeds were milling around a water tank that was supplied by a windmill pump.

A few yards in front of her and Charlie, Roy twisted around in his saddle. "We'll ride to the water tank," he told Justine. "Or are you getting too tired?"

His consideration both touched and surprised her. She hadn't expected her comfort to cross his mind. "I'm fine, and Marble seems fine."

Roy looked at the boy. "How about you, Charlie? Ready to stop?"

"No, sir!"

"Okay. We'll go on to the water tank and let the horses drink, then take a different trail back to the house."

Several minutes later, they reached the cattle. The herd hardly noticed their presence. Roy had to yell out a few yips and wave his arm to clear the three of them a path to the watering tank.

Once there, Roy dismounted, then lifted Charlie out of the saddle. Justine also slid to the ground, and led Marble up to the cool water. Roy and Charlie brought their mounts up beside hers.

"You have a beautiful ranch, Roy," Justine told him as they waited for the three horses to get their fill of water. "How much farther south does it go?"

"Oh, about five more miles, I'd say. The Pardee is big. But not nearly as big as the Bar M."

Lifting her hand to shade her eyes, Justine surveyed the far horizon. She loved this desert land, and was constantly awed by is tough beauty.

"It might not be as big, but I'm sure it's more solvent."

Roy looked at her sharply. "What are you saying? That the Bar M is in financial trouble?"

Justine made a dismissive gesture with her hand. "It's not exactly in trouble," she said, wishing she'd kept her thoughts to herself. She, and her family, didn't necessarily want anyone to know about their financial woes. "Things have been a little strained since Daddy died, that's all. Of course, it sure would help if the cattle market would come out of its slump."

"If prices stay this low for very long, the little fellows will be forced out of business," he agreed. "But you Murdock sisters aren't a little operation. You'll make it."

Justine appreciated his confidence, but she wasn't so certain herself. She knew Rose was definitely unsettled by the Bar M's lack of working funds.

The ride back to the ranch took nearly an hour. By that time, Justine was beginning to get saddle-sore.

"Your walk appears to be a little stiff," Roy remarked to Justine as they left the corrals and headed to the house.

"I don't ride every day, like my sisters and Charlie do," she said, then smiled at the sight of her son loping far ahead of them. "Look at him. He had enough energy to go another five miles."

"I'll bet he could go that far and more," Roy agreed, then slanted her a glance. "I don't guess you've ever regretted having him? I mean, even though you've had to raise him all alone?"

Justine kept her gaze firmly on Charlie. "There was no anguished choice for me when I discovered I was pregnant," she told him truthfully. "I knew I wanted him or her. I loved my child before it was born, and now...well, Charlie is everything to me."

Like a lance thrown by an angry hand, jealousy tore a hole through Roy's chest. He knew it was foolish to feel that way, but he couldn't seem to stop the evil green emotion from spreading through him. Over and over through the years, he'd found himself wishing that it had been Justine, instead of Marla, who came to him with the news that she was pregnant with his child.

And now that Justine had returned home and he'd met Charlie, he wished it a thousand times more. Yet he couldn't change the past. He had to think about the future.

This morning, before their ride, he'd told Justine that his invitation was prompted solely by his wish for Charlie to see the paints. But that hadn't been entirely true. He might as well admit it to himself.

For the past several months, Roy had been feeling flat, although he didn't know why. He served the county as sheriff and then he came home and took care of the ranching chores. He had plenty of things to keep him busy and his mind occupied. But in spite of that, he'd been thinking, brooding, wondering if there was supposed to be more to life than what he had.

Then he'd been called to the Bar M and Justine had opened the door. The moment he saw her, it had been as though scales had fallen from his eyes. Everything around him had seemed sharper, more vibrant. He'd felt more alive than he had in months. She did that to him. She was like a light in the darkness.

"Justine?"

"Yes."

"This morning, when you questioned me about asking you over here today, I...well, the answer I gave you wasn't entirely honest."

Her heart beating fast, she turned her head to look at him.

"No?"

The twist of his lips was full of self-disgust. "As you've probably already guessed, I'm not a sociable sort of guy. My work keeps me pretty busy."

"I'm sure it does."

"I don't get to...have much company. There's never anyone around that I can just talk to about things that have nothing to do with the law. I guess I just wanted someone to talk to."

More than anything Roy had ever said to her, these words shook her, turned her insides to warm mush. "And you wanted that someone to be me?"

The dismay in her voice put a wry smile on his face. "Why should that surprise you? We've known each other a long time, and I consider you a friend."

Perhaps Justine should have been insulted that he considered her a friend, rather than an old flame. But she wasn't. A friend was special. And whether she wanted to admit it to herself or not, that was what she wanted to be to Roy. Special.

Justine and Roy had reached the yard. Charlie came racing from the front of the house to join up with the two adults.

"When are we gonna eat?" he asked.

"Eat? Charlie, you're not supposed to invite yourself to eat at someone else's house," Justine gently scolded him.

"But we need to have a cookout," he explained. "That's what cowboys do when they get back from a long ride."

Roy laughed while Justine groaned.

"He's been watching too much of that western channel," she said.

Snagging his thumbs over the waistband of his jeans, Charlie rocked back on his heels and looked up at Roy. "Do you know what a cookout is?"

Roy pretended to mull over Charlie's question. "I think I do. I don't have a chuck wagon, though. But I have a grill, and plenty of mesquite."

"Do you have steak and beans?" Charlie asked.

Roy chuckled. "I might find steaks in the freezer and a can of pintos in the cupboard. Can you help me get the fire going?"

Charlie literally bounced on his toes. "I sure can!"

Justine quickly spoke up before the two of them could make more plans. "Oh, we'll not be staying to eat, Roy. We need to be getting home. I have a jillion things to do, and Kitty might be needing help with the twins."

He guided her up a short set of steps and onto a redwood deck. "You two have to eat sometime, and so do I. It wouldn't be very hospitable of me to allow you to go home hungry."

When Justine drove over here this morning, she'd expected to stay for only a few short minutes and then be gone. Taking a long horseback ride, then sharing a meal with Roy, was the last thing she'd planned on doing today. But what the heck, she decided. For once, the man was being more like the Roy she used to know, and she couldn't resist spending a bit more time with him.

"Well, I suppose Charlie and I could help you scrape something together," she told him.

They entered the house, and Justine quickly ushered Charlie to the bathroom, where she ordered him to wash. Once he was finished and out of the small room, she used the facilities herself, then went back to the kitchen to see if there was anything she could do to help Roy with the meal.

She found the room empty. However, there were three steaks thawing in the microwave and two cans of beans sitting on the cabinet counter. He obviously intended to give Charlie the meal he wanted.

Deciding that for the moment there was nothing for her to do in the kitchen, Justine started to the back door, then stopped when she heard Roy and Charlie's voices on the deck.

Peering through the screen, she could see the two of them filling a grill with mesquite chips.

"That's enough," Roy said as he eyed the measure of wood.

Grinning impishly, Charlie added one more to the pile, and for a moment Justine thought he might scold their son. As she'd said earlier, in the barn, Roy wasn't softhearted enough to spoil.

But to Justine's surprise, Roy chuckled and ruffled the top of Charlie's head. "All right. One more. But no more. Do you want to squirt the lighter fluid on the wood?"

"Yeah!" Charlie exclaimed. "Can I put the match on it, too?"

Roy shook his head. "No. You're going to stand far back when I do that. Understand?"

Not the least bit disappointed, Charlie nodded. "Yes, sir! I'll get back, 'cause I don't want my eyelashes singed."

Roy glanced at the boy. "Have you ever had your eyelashes singed?"

Charlie's head swung back and forth. "Nope. But Mommy has. She got too close when she was building a fire in the fireplace."

"Your mommy needs to be more careful. We wouldn't want anything to happen to her."

Justine's heart felt as if it were tearing into jagged pieces. As she took in the sight of her son and his father, it almost seemed as if the three of them were a real family. But they weren't, and she'd be crazy to ever think they could be.

Misty-eyed, Justine continued to watch the two of them until the fire was burning and they started back into the house.

Quickly stepping away from the door, she went over to the cabinet counter and began opening the cans of beans.

"Is everything going all right in here?" Roy asked.

Sniffing, she plastered a smile on her face, then glanced over her shoulder at him. "Sure. Did you get the fire started?"

Charlie, who'd sidled up to Roy, gave his mother a proud nod. "We sure did."

Roy patted the top of his head. "My sidekick here did most of the work."

As Charlie continued to beam from ear to ear, Justine knew that this outing today with Roy was one her son would never forget. And she was glad that he was having this bit of time with his father, even if it might be the only time.

"Will it be long till the food is ready?" Charlie asked.

Justine nodded. "You'll have to find something to do until the steaks cook."

"I'll go play with Levi."

"Wait a minute," Roy told him. He walked over to the cabinets and pulled a mangled rubber ball from a drawer. Handing it to Charlie, he said, "Levi loves to play fetch. The farther you throw it, the better he likes it."

"What if I throw the ball so far Levi can't find it?"

Roy chuckled and gave Justine a sidelong wink. "Don't worry, partner, Levi has a nose like a hound. He'll sniff the ball out no matter where you throw it."

"Boy! He must be some dog. I'm gonna try it!"

"Just stay away from the river," Justine cautioned him.

"I know, Mommy. I will."

Charlie raced out the screen door and off the deck. Justine gave Roy a wry smile. "I guess you can tell he's enjoying himself."

"He doesn't appear to be bored."

Now that Charlie had gone outside, the kitchen seemed much smaller. Her heart began to thud faster, and every nerve in her body tightened with anticipation. Of what, she didn't quite know. She only knew that the sight of Roy's hard, masculine body standing so near to her was a temptation she wasn't used to dealing with.

"Charlie loves doing anything outdoors," she told him. "Especially if it involves horses or dogs."

A faint smile touched his face. "You know, I never thought I liked children that much. I didn't know what they were like, and I wasn't sure I cared to know. But after being around Charlie and the twins—''

He took a deep breath, then let it out slowly. Justine got the impression he was embarrassed by his newfound feelings. But that wasn't surprising. Roy had always been... maybe not a macho man, but a tough man's man. She supposed it was a surprise to him to discover he had a soft spot for little ones. It certainly surprised her.

''You realize how special they are,'' she finished for him.

He nodded. ''Yeah. I guess that's what I'm trying to say.''

Not stopping to question herself, she closed the small space between them and laid her hand on his forearm. ''Feeling tender toward children doesn't make you any less of a man, Roy. Only more.''

He looked down at her small, soft hand, curled around his arm. It felt so good to have her touching him like this, to know she'd done it of her own accord and not because he'd riled her into it.

''Well, I don't figure it makes much difference. I doubt I'll ever have any children of my own.''

Now is the time, Justine, a voice inside her whispered loudly. Tell him about Charlie. Tell him that he already has a son.

As the urging of the voice swirled around in her head, something else hit her, something so strong and overwhelming, she couldn't stop herself from inching closer and lifting her face up to his.

''Roy, I—'' She stopped as all sorts of words tangled in a confused wad on her tongue. She was full of the need to give to him, yet terrified that she had nothing he wanted from her. ''Kiss me, will you?''

She could see a look of surprise flicker in his eyes, and then, suddenly, it didn't matter that she was behaving recklessly. His mouth settled over hers, and sweet contentment poured through her body, urged her onto her tiptoes and her arms around his lean waist.

He kissed her not for just a moment, but for a long time. With one hand on her face and the other threaded through the hair above her ear, he tasted every curve of her lips, explored the sharp edge of her teeth with his tongue.

Justine's palms slid up his chest, then settled around the hard muscles of his neck. He felt warm and wonderful and so right. And as Justine gave her mouth to him, she realized she'd only just now come home to the Hondo Valley. She knew in the deepest part of her that Roy was the only man who could make her feel this way, the only man she would ever want to love her like this.

Roy finally lifted his head and gazed down at her. Caressing her cheek with his thumb, he said in a thick voice, "It's been a long time since I've had an invitation like that from you."

Now that there was a bit of space between them, the reality of what she'd just done hit Justine like an avalanche. She'd more or less told him she wanted him. Dear Lord, what must he be thinking?

Color swept across her cheeks, and her eyes dropped to the center of his chest. "Yes. A long time," she agreed, her voice low and husky.

"You probably don't want to tell me why, do you?"

"Why?" she asked shakily.

His thumb slid beneath her chin and tilted her face up to his searching eyes. "Why you wanted me to kiss you."

Now that sanity had crept back in, Justine felt like an idiot. So what if she still loved Roy? That didn't mean he had any sort of feelings toward her. Other than friendship, she told herself. But friends didn't kiss. Not the way Roy had just kissed her.

"No," she said.

He grimaced, and she threw up her hands in a gesture of surrender. "Oh, all right. You're a good-looking man,

Roy. You know that without me telling you. And I was simply tempted by the sight of you.''

He didn't appear to be a bit convinced. ''My looks are the same as they were a few days ago, and you sure as heck weren't inviting me to kiss you then. In fact, you insisted you didn't like my company.''

Annoyed with herself more than with him, she twisted away from the hold he had on her waist and walked over to the screen door. ''I know you're the sheriff, but do you interrogate every woman who invites you to kiss her?''

Frowning, he said, ''I know you won't believe this, but you're the only woman who's issued such an invitation to me.''

She grunted mockingly. ''You're right, I don't believe it.'' Whirling back around to him, she said, ''Roy, I wish you'd forget the whole thing. Women have urges, just like men do. I had an urge, nothing more.''

She knew she was making herself sound cheap, but that was better than confessing that she loved him. He didn't want to hear it, and she didn't want to give him the opportunity to throw her heart back in her face.

Roy didn't believe her. Justine wasn't the sort of woman who kissed a man without some sort of feeling behind it. But he wasn't going to push the issue any further. He wasn't sure he wanted to know what had motivated her to suddenly melt in his arms. He liked being around Justine and he liked being around Charlie. But he didn't want to get to liking their company too much. Marla had betrayed him. Justine had walked out on him. He didn't ever want to go through that much pain again. But, dear God, a moment ago it had felt like heaven to have her back in his arms. He hated these swiftly changing feelings he'd been having ever since he'd seen Justine again.

''Don't worry, Roy,'' Justine went on, when he continued to remain silent. ''I promise not to get any more urges around you. It was just a onetime thing.''

Roy wasn't at all sure that was the sort of promise he wanted from her. "You certainly know how to toy with a man's ego. First you ask him to kiss you, and then you tell him it'll never happen again. I feel like a balloon that's lost its hot air."

Relief swept through Justine. Apparently he'd decided not to take her kiss seriously. Smiling now, she said, "I'm sure your ego is just fine. Now, don't you think we should check on the fire? I'm sure the steaks are thawed and ready to cook."

Seeing she was determined to drop the whole thing, he nodded. "You're right. Charlie's going to be yelling he's starving."

Roy stepped past her and out the door. Closing her eyes, Justine remained where she stood and tried to collect her scattered senses.

Kitty was right. She still loved Roy. So what was she going to do now?

More than an hour later, the three of them had finished a meal of steak, beans and tossed salad. Beneath the shade of a cottonwood, Justine and Roy sat in lawn chairs, drinking coffee. Charlie sat on the ground near their feet as he painstakingly pulled sandburs from Levi's fur.

"Charlie, I think you and I should help Roy clean the table, then go home," Justine told him. "It's going to be time for you to help Aunt Chloe with the chores."

Twisting around, he frowned at his mother. "Aw, Aunt Chloe is all fired up over the twins. She won't even notice I'm not there."

With arched brows, Justine studied her son. As yet, he hadn't shown any jealousy over the twins. He seemed to adore them. Wanting to stay here with Roy was more likely the reason her son was whining.

"You know that isn't true, Charlie. Aunt Chloe will be

expecting you to feed and water Thundercloud and help her with the other horses.''

The boy reluctantly got to his feet. "I guess you're right," he mumbled.

He obviously wasn't ready to leave Roy's company, and Justine began to wonder if she'd only set her son up for future disappointment. Roy might not feel inclined to invite her and Charlie to his ranch again. And even if he did, she wasn't sure she should come back. With or without her son. Being with Roy was only going to feed her love for him.

Before she could go any further, Roy answered one of her questions.

"Maybe your mother will bring you back sometime soon, Charlie," he suggested to the boy.

Charlie turned eagerly to his mother. "Will you, Mommy? Can we come back and see Roy tomorrow?"

"No. Not tomorrow. Maybe in a few days."

Justine rose to her feet. As she did, a beeping noise sounded somewhere close. She watched Roy pull a pager from under the tail of his shirt and read the number. Apparently he'd been carrying the communication device with him all day but no one had tried to contact him until now.

"Looks like I have to go use the phone," he told Justine. "I'll be back in a minute."

He hurried on into the house. Justine went up on the deck and began to clear away the dishes on the table where they'd eaten their meal.

She was carrying an armload into the kitchen when Roy appeared from another part of the house. He was buckling his pistol around his hips, and the urgency of his movements sent a surge of fear through her.

"Is something wrong?"

He nodded. "A wanted fugitive was spotted traveling on the highway between Tularosa and Mescalero. A deputy tried to pull him over, and a high-speed chase carried them over into Lincoln County where both vehicles wrecked.

Now the deputy is injured and the fugitive is running on foot in the desert.''

"How awful!" Justine responded. "Is he armed?"

"From the brief report I got, he has some sort of handgun," Roy answered as he hurried over to a metal cabinet jammed in a corner next to the refrigerator. Quickly he unlocked it, pulled out a pump shotgun and a box of shells. "I've got to get the hounds and get over there and find him."

Justine crossed the room to him. "*You* have to find him? Why do you have to find him? I thought a sheriff just gave orders and the deputies did the legwork."

He shot her an annoyed look of disbelief. "One deputy has already been hurt. I don't intend to let another be injured."

Justine's eyes widened with fear. "But you might be shot at. You could even be killed by this lunatic!"

With a wry twist to his face, he started out the door. "That's what being the sheriff sometimes means, Justine. See ya later."

By ten o'clock that night, Justine was pacing from one end of the house to the other.

The desert was always a dangerous place to be, especially at night. But Roy was out there tracking down a criminal with a gun. What was happening? she wondered. Was he still out there? Was the hunt over? Had Roy been shot at or hurt?

"Justine, you're walking a hole in the tiles," Kitty said to her niece as she entered the living room. "Why don't you sit down with your sisters?"

Sighing, Justine went over to the couch and sat down beside Rose, who was reading a magazine.

The older Murdock sister glanced up as the cushion next to her sagged with Justine's weight. "You've been restless ever since you came home this evening. What's the matter?" Rose asked.

Chloe spoke up from across the room. "It's the sheriff. I think our sister has fallen for the steely-eyed lawman."

"Hush, Chloe, you don't know what you're talking about," Kitty said sharply.

Both Rose and Chloe looked at their aunt with curious surprise. "What's the matter? I was only teasing my sister a little," Chloe said defensively. "Besides, she did spend most of the day with the man."

Justine pressed her fingers against her closed eyelids. "If you all must know, I'm worried."

"It's the twins," Chloe suddenly said in a panicked rush. "The sheriff has found something out about the babies, and you don't want to tell us!"

"No. It isn't that at all," Justine assured her. Dropping her hands from her face, she glanced at the three women. "Before Charlie and I left Roy's this evening, he was called to work."

Chloe laughed with relief. "And that's what's worrying you? The man is sheriff of Lincoln County, Justine. He has to be available twenty-four hours a day."

Justine glared at her younger sibling. "He's out in the desert, tracking down an armed fugitive."

"Oh, my," Rose said quietly. "What happened?"

Justine recounted the brief details Roy had given her. "It's the not knowing that's worrying me," she finished.

Kitty reached for the remote control to the TV set. "Let's turn on the ten-o'clock news. Maybe they'll have something on the story."

The older woman clicked through the channels until she reached the nearest station to Hondo. The anchorman was giving a brief recount of the world news, and then he turned to local happenings.

"Look, here's the story now," Chloe yelped as a videotape began to show a night scene of patrol cars and lawmen parked along a barren stretch of highway near Oscuro.

Justine scooted to the edge of her seat, her heart pounding, as a young female reporter relayed the bits of information she had gathered so far at the scene.

"Well, we don't really know much more than we did," Kitty said, once the reporter had signed off. "Roy is still out there, and has been for several hours."

"She said shots had been fired," Rose added with concern.

"That could mean anything," Chloe said. She crossed the room to Justine and curled her arm around her shoulders. "Don't worry, sis, Roy Pardee seems like a pretty tough guy to me. And I'm sure he knows what he's doing."

Justine forced herself to nod, but she couldn't rid herself of the icy fear settling in the pit of her stomach. There had been such a hard, determined look in his eyes when he walked out the door.

"Roy isn't a man to back down," she said lowly. "Even if his life is in danger."

"That's what being a sheriff means, Justine," Rose told her matter-of-factly.

Justine looked over at her older sister. "That's what he told me, too. But I guess I never realized exactly what Roy was until this evening. He's the law." Her eyes focused on the dark picture window on the opposite side of the room. Beyond the glass was a view of the Hondo Valley, her home. Roy had sworn to protect not only this place, but all of Lincoln County, a county that had gone down in American history for its bloody range wars. Countless numbers of men had died in shoot-outs on this land. Now Roy was out there, searching for an angry man with a gun. The whole idea left her chilled with fear.

"Justine, do you hear me?"

Finally realizing Chloe was saying something to her, Justine turned her head toward her sister. "What?"

"I was asking just what you were doing over at the sheriff's place all day."

Justine wasn't really in the mood for an interrogation

from her family tonight, but she knew it would look strange if she refused to answer.

She turned her gaze back on the window. "We took Charlie for a horseback ride, then cooked steaks on the grill."

Justine was aware of Chloe and Rose exchanging curious glances.

"Does this mean the man has quit rubbing you the wrong way?" Rose questioned.

"It means I've learned that Roy isn't quite the man I believed him to be six years ago," she said, then quickly rose to her feet. "If you all don't mind, I'm going to bed now."

With her aunt and two sisters staring worriedly after her, Justine left the room and walked down the hallway to Charlie's bedroom.

A night-light was burning near the head of his bed. Justine reached down and tenderly brushed the thick shock of bangs away from his forehead.

He'd been so worn out from his play at Roy's that he nearly fell asleep in the bathtub. And when she tucked him in bed, he'd still been talking about Roy and asking how many days it would be before they could go back to see him.

What if Charlie never got to see his father again? she asked herself. What if Roy was killed, and never knew he had a son?

Maybe her mind was exaggerating the danger Roy was facing. He'd probably even laugh if he knew how worried she was about him. Even so, the questions weighed on her mind like a dark, oppressive storm cloud, and she knew she couldn't go on with all these feelings bottled up and hidden away inside her.

Right or wrong, she had to tell Roy how much she loved him.

Chapter Seven

Justine normally enjoyed her job at the clinic. Dr. Bellamy was kind and considerate with his patients and employees. On many days, the clinic was full and the workday was long and hectic, without a moment to draw an extra breath. Unfortunately, today was a slow one, and Justine had long spells of time on her hands to worry and wonder, to ask herself a thousand times over if she was crazy to let Roy know how she felt about him.

She'd heard, from a talkative patient and Carlita, the receptionist, that Roy had apprehended the fugitive early this morning, before daylight. The prisoner was now in the county jail in Carrizozo. The deputy who had been injured in the high-speed chase was recovering nicely in the hospital.

Everything had turned out all right. Roy was safe. Justine should be relieved, but she wasn't. Last night had proved to her just how much she loved Roy. The thought of not ever seeing him again, not hearing his voice or touching his face, was too horrific to contemplate. She wanted to be a part of his life. It was that simple and that terrifying.

Just before Justine's workday ended, she called Kitty and told her she wouldn't be coming home straightaway, then dialed the sheriff's office in Carrizozo.

A sleepy-voiced deputy answered the phone. "Yes, Sheriff Pardee is in his office," he told Justine, "but he's busy. Maybe I can help you with your problem?"

"No. I'm afraid not—I need to speak to Roy about something personal."

The deputy cleared his throat. When he spoke again, Justine could hear a wide smile in his voice. Obviously he thought it amusing that a woman was calling his boss. "Oh, I see," he said. "So who should I tell him is calling?"

"Justine."

"Okay, Justine. I'll see what I can do."

The line was silent only a few seconds before Roy picked up the phone.

"Justine? Is something wrong?"

The sound of his voice was so precious that tears of relief suddenly filled her eyes and knotted her throat. "No. There's nothing wrong," she answered quickly.

"You don't sound like yourself."

She was more herself, Justine realized, than she had been in years. Six years, to be exact.

"I'm…fine. I was calling because…I was worried about you."

There was a long pause, and she knew her admission had probably knocked a bit of wind from him. Finally she heard him speaking to someone who must have been in the room with him.

"Don't you have something to do, Randall? Get out of here. Go wash your patrol car!" To Justine he said, in a softer tone, "There's no need for you to be worried. I'm fine. The job is done. The prisoner is in jail."

She let out a long breath. "I'm glad. I've had all sorts of horrible thoughts running through my head since you left the ranch yesterday."

To know that Justine had been thinking of him, worrying about him, did strange things to Roy. His job had put him in many dangerous situations before, but those who knew him never worried about him. They thought he was tough and invincible. They considered him a survivor, a sheriff who always won out in the end like Matt Dillon or Wyatt Earp. But Justine was thinking of him simply as a man, and the idea filled him with an emotion he'd never felt before.

"Did you and Charlie make it back home okay?" he asked.

"Yes. I washed the dishes and locked your house before we left."

"You could have left the dishes for me."

"I wanted to do them for you."

There was something new in her voice, Roy decided, something soft and intimate that pulled and pushed at him. At this moment, he wished he could hold her. But he also wished he didn't want to.

"Are you going to be tied up this evening?" she asked before her courage lagged.

"No. Since I worked all night, I'm heading home early. Why?"

Fatigue was in his voice, and Justine knew that now was probably not the time to be talking to him about anything. But the urge to see him if for no other reason than to assure herself that he was all right, was strong.

"I'd like to talk to you."

"You're talking to me now."

She swallowed. "It's not...something I can say over the phone."

"Justine—"

Suddenly she remembered all the times these past few days when he'd called and ordered her about. "Damn it, Roy, don't put me off. Just tell me where to meet you and be there!"

Roy had never had the urge to curse and laugh at the same time, but he did now. "Using my tactics now, are you?"

"You forced me into it."

He let out a rough sigh. "Okay. I've got to eat. I'll meet you in Ruidoso." He named a local café and a time for her to be there.

"You don't have to drive that far out of your way," she countered.

"I thought you wanted to see me," he said impatiently.

"I do!"

"Then why are you arguing with me?"

"I'm not arguing, I'm trying to make it easier for you," she reasoned.

Seeing Justine was always easy on the eyes, but it was never easy on his heart. After yesterday, he was beginning to wonder if inviting her and Charlie to the ranch had been a big mistake. He'd liked having them there too much. He'd liked having Justine in his kitchen, and in his arms, kissing him like she never wanted to stop. But stop she would. She had before.

"What do you want, Justine?"

The weariness in his voice stung her. Yet she wanted to cry, "You, Roy. I want you." Instead, she said, "I'll tell you about it when I see you."

Because it was so far from her workplace to the Bar M, Justine kept a couple of changes of clothes at the clinic in case she needed to do something in town and didn't want to look like a nurse while she was doing it.

Before she left the office, she changed into a swingy printed rayon skirt and a cool green tank top, then tied her hair back from her face with a matching green scarf.

When she reached the café, she had several minutes to spare before Roy arrived. She found a table by a window overlooking the woods that crowded up to the back of the building. When a waitress arrived, she ordered iced tea and informed the woman that someone would be meeting her shortly.

While she sipped the drink and watched chipmunks chase around the pine trunks, the bell over the door jangled several times. Each time it sounded, Justine glanced around, expecting to see Roy, and each time was ridiculously disappointed when it wasn't.

She had very nearly finished her tea and was about to glance at her watch again when footsteps sounded behind her.

"Hello, Justine."

She looked over her shoulder at him, and her heart caught in her throat. His face was unshaven, his blue eyes were bloodshot and his clothes were stained with dirt and dried sweat. He looked rough and rugged and so very weary. But he'd never looked better to her than he did at this moment. It was all she could to keep from rising to her feet and flinging her arms around his neck.

"Thank you for coming, Roy."

He pulled out a chair and sat down a few inches away from her. His nearness very nearly took her breath away, and she wondered how she had existed these past six years without him. Moreover, she wondered how she would be able to exist the next six if he rejected her.

"Well, you were persistent, and I am hungry. Are you?"

Surprisingly, she was hungry, now that he was here with her. "Yes, I could eat something."

As if on cue, a waitress arrived at their table. "Do you need to see menus?" the woman asked.

Roy glanced questioningly at Justine. "I'll have whatever you're having," she told him.

Without bothering to read the menu, he ordered for both of them. The waitress left, then immediately returned with a cup of coffee for Roy and a refill of Justine's iced tea.

Once she moved away from their table, a long stretch of awkward silence ensued. After a while, Justine could feel

Roy's eyes moving over her face and hair and down to the thrust of her breasts. The caress of his gaze left her more than warm, and she wondered if he was looking to purposely disturb her, or if he was looking because he actually wanted to.

"You didn't want to see me this evening," she said flatly, her eyes on the amber liquid swirling around her glass.

He made a small sound of disbelief in his throat. "I never said anything to give you that impression. Besides, there isn't a man breathing that wouldn't enjoy seeing you."

She smiled at him. "You still are a flirt, Roy Pardee," she said softly, as her eyes drifted over the tired lines of his face. "That hasn't changed about you."

The corners of his mouth tilted into a semblance of a grin. "I'm not flirting, just stating a fact."

She wanted to lean her face into his and kiss him so badly that she ached from the effort of stopping herself.

Glancing away from him, she said, "Charlie is still talking about you. He thinks you're the greatest thing to happen since Roy Rogers and Trigger."

Roy chuckled. "Isn't Roy Rogers and Trigger a little outdated for Charlie? I thought kids nowadays were infatuated with those space-age cartoons and character figures that are on TV."

Justine shook her head. "Not Charlie. He likes fast-ropin', hard-ridin' shoot-'em-up cowboys, like the Durango Kid."

Roy smiled wryly as he lifted his coffee cup to his lips. "My kind of boy."

Justine's heart pained at his innocent remark. Charlie *was* his boy. The question now wasn't if she was going to tell him. It was when and how. She didn't want Roy to know Charlie was his son until she could be sure how he really felt about her. She wanted him to love and want her solely for herself, and not because she was the mother of his son.

And if he said he could never love her? Well, she'd just have to take things from there, she supposed.

"So did you want to talk to me about Charlie? Is that what this is all about?" he asked.

She glanced sharply at him. "No."

"The twins?"

Justine shook her head. She didn't want to get into this now, with a roomful of people sitting only a few steps away.

"The twins are fine. Chloe and Rose are smitten with the babies."

"And you are, too."

She made a yielding gesture with her hand, then smiled guiltily. "Well, yes, I guess I'm pretty much taken with them, too."

His expression grew serious. His eyes soft. "You were meant to be a mother, Justine. I can see that now. I couldn't see it six years ago."

"You were young."

"I wanted you. Only you."

The directness of his words, the dark, brooding shadows suddenly filling his eyes, left Justine's whole insides trembling. She was almost glad the waitress chose that moment to arrive with their food.

They ate a platter of enchiladas and Spanish rice, then finished the meal with a basket of sopaipillas and more coffee.

By the time the two of them left the small café, the sky had grown dark and a chill had replaced the heat of the day.

Justine hugged her arms against her as they walked silently across the parking lot. Once they reached the truck she'd driven, Roy caught her lightly by the waist.

"Okay, I got the idea you didn't want to tell me what was on your mind in there while we were eating," he said. "So tell me now."

Her eyes wide, she glanced around them. "Here?"

He looked as if he were annoyed and tired and fast losing his patience. "What more do you want, Justine? We don't have an audience. It's just you and me. If it's confidential—"

"I love you."

Roy's head reared back as if she'd slapped him in the mouth. "You what?"

She breathed a ragged breath in and out, and was vaguely aware of his grip tightening on both sides of her waist.

"You heard me. I said I love you."

His expression incredulous, he stared at her. "Justine... Oh, hell!"

Grabbing her by the arm, he led her away from the truck and into the dark woods behind the café. Once they were out of sight, he pushed her up against the trunk of a huge pine and pinned her there with his hands on both her shoulders.

"What do you mean, blurting out something like that to me?" She'd stunned him, knocked the very wind from his chest.

Her heart was pounding so hard and fast she thought it was going to burst. "What more did you want?" she asked, tossing his own words back at him. "Wine, roses and romance? We had our time for that six years ago, Roy. If you think I was too blunt, I'm sorry. If you didn't want to hear how I feel about you, I'm sorry about that, too. But I had to tell you."

His eyes narrowed as they bored into hers. He desperately wanted to believe her, but he didn't want to be her fool a second time. "What kind of game are you playing with me, Justine?"

He wasn't happy. But then, she should have known he wouldn't be. He'd already implied that he wasn't in the market for love or marriage. But when he kissed her, she'd felt a need in him, a need that matched the one in her heart.

And she'd hoped that maybe, deep down, he did care for her.

"I don't play games, Roy."

"That's what it looks like to me. You've played Miss Ice Maiden ever since that night you discovered the twins and called me out to the ranch."

"That's not true," she shot back.

"And now you say you love me," he said, his voice dripping with sarcasm. "We're not teenagers anymore, Justine. You can't just spout off words and expect me to believe them. Especially when you think it might be convenient for you."

"Convenient!" She gasped with outrage and shoved hard against his shoulders. He didn't budge. "How dare you say that to me! I'm not asking anything from you. I don't—I didn't really expect anything from you. Six years ago, you didn't care about me, and it's obvious you still don't. Now let me go!"

When he didn't release his grip on her shoulders, she stomped on the toe of his boot. The surprise attack caused his hold to loosen. Justine twisted away and began to run.

"Damn it all! Justine come back here!"

Ignoring his call, she darted through the pines and back toward the incline leading up to the parking lot. However, just before she left the shelter of the trees, Roy caught up to her and snaked an arm around her waist.

With a quick little jerk, he spun her around and into his arms.

"What are you trying to do to me?" He growled the question only inches away from her lips.

Her breast heaving, her whole body shaking, Justine stared up and into his eyes. "I'm not trying to do anything to you! I don't *want* to do anything to you!"

"You're lying!" She wanted him as much as he wanted her. Why couldn't she admit it?

Justine raised her hands to break free of him, but she

never had the chance to follow through. Her lips were suddenly captured beneath his. Squirming, she tried to pull away from him, but his hand was at the back of her head, making it impossible for her to escape his kiss.

Just when she'd decided he meant only to punish her, the pressure of his mouth eased and his fingers tangled loosely in her hair, while the arm around her waist slid upward against her back.

As he drew her closer, Justine groaned and parted her lips. He tasted them hungrily, thrust his tongue between her teeth and explored the ribbed roof of her mouth.

In spite of his jaded reaction to her declaration of love, Justine couldn't stop the desire she felt for him. She couldn't stop her body from arching into his and silently begging him to make love to her.

"This is what you want," he mouthed roughly against her lips. "It's what I want."

"Roy, this isn't—"

His hand cupped around her face. His forefinger pressed against the corner of her lips. "Don't talk. You've already said too much."

She wanted to hit him, yell at him that he didn't have any idea what she really wanted from him. But, for the moment, the need to make love to him, to have him make love to her, was outweighing everything.

His lips pressed a kiss beneath her ear, then traveled down the side of her neck. "You—don't know anything, Roy," she said between groans.

"Oh, yes. I do know. You've been asking for this much, at least, and I'm going to give it to you," he murmured as hot desire surged through his body.

His head dipped lower, and she gasped as his teeth sank into the fabric of her blouse, then found the peak of her breast. Heat poured through her like a wild rainstorm, and she realized that a part of what Roy had said was true. She did want this. She wanted his lips on hers, his hands on her breast, his hips grinding rhythmically against hers. It was decadent and crazy. But in her heart, he'd always been her lover, and he always would be.

It was Roy who finally stepped back from her. By then, Justine's senses were reeling, and she unconsciously gripped his arm for support.

"No matter what you're thinking, Roy," she whispered, "I didn't come here tonight for this."

Glancing away from her, he lifted his Stetson from his head and ran his hand through his hair. Justine thought she saw a trembling in his fingers. But that could hardly be. The sheriff of Lincoln County didn't fear anything. He didn't *feel* anything. Not that much.

"What did you come for?" he asked in an accusing voice. "To see if you could make my resistance crumble? To see if you could still turn me inside out?"

With a self-mocking groan, Justine turned her back on him. "There's no point in me trying to answer your question. Last night I was so frightened for you, so terrified that you might be hurt or killed. But a person without a heart can't understand something like that. You can't understand what it's like to love someone."

"Love—" He snorted as he remembered the pain he'd went through when she'd walked out on him. "Don't ever talk to me about love. I don't believe in it."

"Don't worry, Roy, you won't ever hear the word from me again," she said in choked voice. Then, before he could stop her, she ran to the parking lot and climbed into her truck.

Her hands were shaking so badly, she fumbled the key several times before she finally twisted it enough to start the motor. By then, Roy was stepping out of the woods and onto the parking lot.

Justine didn't wait around to see if he was headed her way. She jerked the truck into reverse and backed onto the main highway. Once she was headed east, she stepped down hard on the accelerator, squealing tires as she went. If he wanted to get her for reckless driving, then he damn well could. But she'd had all the rejection she could stand for one night.

"Fred, are you sure this is the woman you saw with the twins? Is it a good likeness of her?" Roy asked the burly man sitting across the booth from him.

Fred carefully studied the composite drawing. "Looks like her to me."

Roy nodded. "Good. I'm going to spread this around and see what happens."

"You know, that's a strange thing, them babies showing up at the Murdock ranch like that. What do you think it's all about, Roy?"

Roy's face hardened. "I think it's about a mother who doesn't want her children."

Fred shook his head in disgust. "If that's the case, it seems to me those two babies would be a lot better off with that pretty nurse you had in here with you the other day. She'd love that little girl and guy with all her heart. You can tell she's just that kinda woman."

Yeah, Roy thought, she was that kinda woman where babies and children were concerned. But what about men? What about him? All she did was confuse him, enrage him...tempt him.

"Yes. She and her sisters are taking good care of them for the time being."

"Well, I hope you find the mother. And when you do, give her a boot in the you-know-what."

Roy picked up the stack of papers with the mystery woman's face printed on the front and rose to his feet. "I'll have to leave her punishment up to the judge, Fred. But I know what you're saying. Thanks for your help."

"No problem. And when you see that pretty nurse again, tell her I said hello."

If the woman who'd dumped the twins was anything like Justine, Roy would have already caught her, he thought. Dozens of men here in Ruidoso would remember turning to look at her. She had that kind of beauty and feminine aura. He knew because he was bewitched by it, despite himself.

"Sure. I'll tell her," Roy promised, then left the ice-cream parlor.

Outside, he climbed into his Bronco, then sat with his hands on the steering wheel and stared unseeingly out the windshield.

It had been a week since he met Justine here in Ruidoso for supper. A week since she blurted out that she loved him. He hadn't seen or talked to her since. And he was miserable.

He missed her terribly. He wanted to hear her voice, see her face, hold her against him. He wanted to tell her he loved her.

Oh, yes, he thought with wry self-mockery, he loved Justine. Even though he'd vowed that he didn't believe in the word, and even though she'd trampled his heart six years ago, he loved her. And he supposed he always had. Why else was she still so much a part of him? Why else did it feel as natural as coming home whenever he touched her?

But not even knowing how he felt about Justine convinced him that the two of them should be together. It didn't convince him of anything except that he was headed for a heartache. Justine didn't believe he had a heart. But he did. It had ached all week. And he wasn't at all sure what to do to make it stop.

He wanted to trust Justine, to believe she would never walk out on him again. But he'd learned the hard way that trusting a woman was risky business.

Muttering a curse under his breath, Roy started the

Bronco and pulled out onto the busy street. If he hurried, he could catch Justine before she left the clinic to go home.

Justine needed to go to the grocery store. In fact, it was a must. The twins were getting low on formula and diapers. Kitty needed several things for the kitchen. Since Justine was the one who worked in town, she usually got the shopping chores.

Normally Justine didn't mind going to the grocery store or running other errands. But today had been one of Dr. Bellamy's busy days. She was exhausted, and she wasn't in the mood to do anything but go home and go to bed.

Admit it, she told herself as she stepped into a pair of black jeans. It isn't your job that's getting you down. It was Roy. More than a dozen times this week, she'd come close to calling him. But each time, she'd stopped herself.

Roy didn't want anything to do with her, and she wasn't going to push herself at him. The spark between them— and that was all it had been, she thought dismally—was all over. As for Charlie, she could hardly see how Roy could love the boy, when he couldn't even bring himself to love his son's mother. And she was relieved she hadn't gone so far as to tell him he was the father of her child. Roy wouldn't have wanted to hear that any more than he wanted to hear that she loved him.

After pulling on a white cotton sweater, she slipped her feet into a pair of leather loafers and left the little makeshift dressing room without bothering to glance in the mirror.

As she passed the front desk, she bade Carlita goodbye, then stepped outside under the awning sheltering the entrance of the building. The leftover remnants of an afternoon rainstorm still lingered over the mountains. Water dripped from the awning and nearby spruce trees as a cool drizzle continued to fall.

Justine dashed to her truck, and was about to open the

door when a hand came from behind and clamped around her wrist.

Gasping, she whirled around, and very nearly collided into Roy's chest.

"Come with me."

He never knew how to ask, only order, Justine thought. Glaring at him, she tried to jerk her hand free of his. "I don't want to come with you!"

His face like granite, he tugged her over to his Bronco and opened the door. "Get in!"

"Are you arresting me?" she asked dryly.

"If necessary." He nudged her toward the vehicle.

Justine reluctantly climbed in and settled herself in the passenger seat. While she waited for him to skirt around the hood and take his seat behind the wheel, she glanced curiously around the cab.

The vehicle was fitted with all sorts of radio and communication devices. High-powered rifles were attached to a mesh partition directly behind their seats. A pair of handcuffs dangled next to them. The sight of the weapons brought the hard reality of Roy's job home to her and made her shiver against the leather seat. She didn't think she could bear it if something happened to Roy in the line of duty.

Roy slid behind the wheel and slammed the door behind him.

When he looked at her and said nothing, Justine's heart began its old familiar thud of love. She tried her best to ignore it.

"Since you're not into social calls, I suppose there's some reason for this visit," she said.

He handed her a copy of the composite drawing. "Fred, you remember the witness at the ice-cream parlor? He's met with the artist from the Albuquerque Police Department. This is what the two of them came up with."

Forgetting her misery for the moment, Justine carefully

studied the woman's face. "I wish I could say she looked familiar. But she doesn't. Not at all."

"Fred says it's a close likeness. I don't know, everyone sees things differently."

How well she knew that, Justine thought. She saw love as something precious and wonderful. Roy saw it as an illusion, a reason to slip a noose around his neck.

"At least it's a start," Justine said.

She offered the paper back to him. He shook his head. "Keep it and show it to your family. Maybe, by some slim chance, one of them might remember seeing her."

"All right." She folded the paper and stuffed it into her clutch bag.

"I've had a deputy searching through local birth records to see who might have had twins in the last five or six months, and where. So far, we've found one set and they're living with their parents in Alto."

"Do you think the twins were born locally? Or at least in the county?"

He shrugged. "We're looking in the county first. If we don't come up with something there, we'll branch out farther."

As they talked, Roy's eyes softened. She could feel them skimming over her face, exploring her lips.

Unsettled by his gaze, she turned her attention out the windshield. "What about my cousins? Have you found either of them yet?"

"The male. Not the female."

"And?"

"You were right. There's not much chance of his involvement. However, we won't rule out his sister until we talk with her."

She wanted him to find the twins' mother, if not for their sake, then at least for Rose and Chloe, who were becoming more and more attached to the babies with each passing day. Yet, at this very moment, discussing the case of the twins was not what she really wanted.

More than anything, Justine longed to ask him if he'd been happy this week. Was he glad he no longer had to worry about her embarrassing him with declarations of love?

"Well," she said as she drew in a painful breath. "If that's all, I'd better be on my way. I have several chores to do before I leave town."

She reached for the door handle.

"Justine?"

She didn't look at him. If she did, tears would fill her eyes, and she couldn't let him see how much he was hurting her.

"Yes?"

She heard him sigh. "How are the twins?"

"They're doing great. I think they've both gained weight. Adam is trying his best to crawl. Though Anna isn't quite so sure about that much traveling yet."

"And Charlie? How is he?"

He couldn't know how much his question crushed her. She loved Charlie so much. For years now, she'd wanted him to have a father. And after seeing Roy again, she'd let herself hope that her son might get to have his real father in his life. But now that would never be.

"Charlie is fine."

"He— Has he asked about me?" He couldn't admit to himself, much less to Justine how much he'd missed Charlie. And her.

She gripped her purse as though it were a lifeline. "He wants to know why we can't go see you. I told him you're busy."

"Not that busy."

Her throat began to ache. She swallowed and forced herself to look at him. "I don't want you to see him anymore."

"Why?"

"I don't want him hurt."

He frowned. "Who says I'd hurt him? I'd never do anything to make that boy unhappy."

"I'm not saying you would. Deliberately. But I don't want to take the chance."

His face hardened. "You think I'm heartless."

She shook her head. "No. I *know* you are."

He muttered a curse.

Justine bit down on her lip as tears blurred her eyes. "I wasn't asking anything from you the other night, Roy. But you... It made you angry to hear me say I love you."

His head whipped around, and his blue eyes glittered as they pinned hers. "You're damn right it made me angry. I don't want you to love me. I don't want to love you."

Rather than let him see her tears, she closed her eyes. "Well, you certainly don't have to worry about that."

Suddenly his hands were on her shoulders, jerking her forward. Her eyes flew open, and she discovered that his face was only inches away from hers.

"How can you be so blind, Justine?"

"I don't know," she mumbled miserably. "I should have realized six years ago that you could never love anyone."

He gave her shoulders a little shake. "I loved you then and I love you now."

She shook her head in disbelief. "Don't lie to me, Roy. I can take anything but that."

His face softened, and his hand gently touched her face. "I wish I was lying. But I'm not. I think of you, I look at you, and my legs turn to two pieces of licorice."

"That's not love. That's lust."

His fingers threaded through her fiery red hair. "I know the difference, Justine."

Her teary eyes filled with sadness. "You love me, but you don't want to. Is that what you're trying to tell me?"

His big hand closed around her chin. "I'm trying like

hell not to love you," he murmured, but his trying was in vain. Every time he touched her his heart melted all over again.

"Why?"

His brows arched, as though he found her question ludicrous. "Why? Well, Marla manipulated and deceived me. You—"

"Roy—"

"I don't blame you for her faults," he said, interrupting her. "You can't help what she tried to do. But you left me without a word, turned your back on me and ran straight to another man's arms and into his bed. I can't forget that, Justine. And even if I could, I'm not so sure I should. I've been in law enforcement a long time, and the job has taught me a lot about human behavior. People rarely change. Once a criminal, always a criminal."

He was ripping her heart to shreds, and there was nothing she could do about it. He believed she'd loved another man after him. Yet she couldn't tell him any different. He would simply count back the years and months and realize that Charlie was his son.

Would it be so terrible if he did know? Would it make things better? Dear Lord, she desperately needed some answers, she silently prayed.

"I see," she said flatly. "I'm the criminal and you're the innocent victim. I think you'd better open your eyes, Roy. Otherwise, you're going to keep living in a fog."

Anger flared his nostrils and tightened his fingers on her shoulder. "I guess you think you were right to leave me all those years ago."

She pulled away from him and reached for the door latch. "It shouldn't matter to you who was right or wrong anymore. That's all in the past. We can't change it. Instead of looking back, you should be thinking about the future. But I see that you can't."

He didn't try to stop her as she opened the door and

climbed out of the cab. For a moment, Justine stood in the drizzle, looking back at him. There was so much she wanted to say. But she had to keep it all inside. She had to stop and think, to decide what was best for Charlie, who was the real innocent victim in all this.

"You hurt me, Justine. Really hurt me."

"And you hurt me, Roy. But we could make it up to each other. Have you ever thought about that?"

Without waiting for a reply, Justine shut the door, climbed into her own vehicle and drove away.

Roy watched her go, then started the Bronco's engine. But then he sat there for several more minutes. He didn't want to go back to work. He didn't want to go home. Without Justine, none of it mattered. It had taken him a long time to realize that. Now he had to figure out what to do to get himself over her. Or could he ever be over Justine?

Chapter Eight

"Justine? Can you come to the study for a moment? I've found something that—well, it seems rather odd."

Justine turned away from the cabinet counter where she'd been helping Kitty fill bottles with baby formula.

"Sure, Rose." She joined her sister, and the two of them walked down the hallway to the study. Since their father's death, Rose had given up her teaching job at a junior high school in Ruidoso and taken on the responsibility of taking care of the cattle, plus the ranch's bookkeeping. Justine knew her sister worked too hard, and at times she tried to help her with some of the paperwork. "Is one of my entries in the checkbook illegible?"

Rose sighed softly. "No, it's not any of your doing. It's something our father did."

Inside the study, Rose motioned Justine to the big oak desk where the records for the ranch were kept.

"I was looking back through some of the older checks, searching for any that might be tax-deductible for the next quarterly, when I found this."

Rose handed Justine the canceled check. It was written

for several hundred dollars. The space marked Pay to the Order of was empty. When Justine flipped the document over, the endorsement was simply stamped For Deposit Only.

"Well, this isn't so strange," Justine said after a moment. "Daddy probably bought something for the ranch and didn't take the time to fill in the name. You know how he was about paperwork. He didn't like to do it. But he didn't want us messing with it, either."

Rose shook her head. "That's what I thought at first. But something didn't feel quite right about it, so I decided to drag out a box of canceled checks that went even farther back." She picked up a stack of checks from the desk and handed them to Justine. "These are all exactly the same as the one you're holding. No name, no endorsement, and deposited into a bank in Las Cruces."

Justine flipped through the checks, and a sense of foreboding began to come over her. "And they're all made out monthly. As if he were making a payment to someone. It doesn't make sense."

"That's the idea I was getting," Rose said. She sank down into the desk chair and looked worriedly at Justine. "What do you think was going on with our father? Do you think he was paying off a gambling debt and didn't want us know about it?"

Justine continued to study the checks. "I know Daddy liked to gamble on the horses. But he always did that at the track in Ruidoso Downs. I don't think he would have been making outside bets. Especially not this size. These checks add up to several thousand dollars."

"Tell me about it," Rose wearily agreed. "It's no wonder we found the ranch account so low. For some reason, Daddy had been draining it." Her eyes suddenly widened. "You don't think— Could it be possible the money has something to do with the twins?"

Justine rubbed her fingers across the furrows in her fore-head. "How could it?"

Rose shrugged her slender shoulders. "I don't know. But it seems odd that the twins appeared here on the ranch, just out of the blue. And now we find these checks—"

As Rose's suspicions trailed away, Justine went around the desk and pulled a plain envelope from a drawer. Stuffing the checks inside, she started toward the door. "There may not be any connection at all between the twins and the money. But we do need to find out who these checks were written to and for what."

"What are you going to do?" Rose asked.

"I'm going to take these to Roy. He'll know what to do with them."

Surprise lifted Rose from her seat. "You're going over to the Pardee Ranch tonight? I thought you and the sheriff were on the outs?"

Justine shook her head. "Does Aunt Kitty tell you and Chloe everything she thinks?"

"Then you're not on the outs with the sheriff?"

Justine sighed. Nearly a week had passed since she talked to Roy in the clinic parking lot. He hadn't tried to contact her since, and Justine figured he'd probably come to some sort of decision. He'd decided that even though he loved her, he could live without her.

"We're not on the outs, Rose. Roy and I— Well, I guess you could say we understand each other."

"You love him."

Justine was no longer going to deny her feelings for Roy. What point would it serve, she thought dismally. Nodding, she said, "Yes."

"Does he know how you feel about him?"

Her heart aching, Justine gave her older sister a wry smile. "Take my advice, Rose, some men just don't want to be loved."

* * *

After changing into a denim skirt and a sage-green T-shirt, Justine called the sheriff's department in Carrizozo. A dispatcher quickly informed her that Sheriff Pardee had already gone home for the evening.

Justine thanked the woman, then headed to the kitchen, where she found her aunt Kitty and Chloe feeding the twins a bowl of applesauce. Charlie had a chair wedged close to the pair of high chairs, and was happily overseeing the whole event.

"Going somewhere?" Chloe asked, noting the clutch purse in Justine's hand.

Her face grim, Justine said, "I'm going to the Pardee Ranch to see Roy."

Hearing Roy's name mentioned, Charlie quickly jumped down from his chair and ran to his mother. "Can I go, Mommy?"

Justine shook her head. "I'm afraid not, son. It's nearly your bedtime now."

"But I want to see Roy," he complained. "I haven't seen him in a long time."

Justine bent down and hugged his shoulders. It was all she could do to keep from bursting into tears in front of Charlie and the rest of her family. "I know it's been a long time since you've seen Roy. But tonight wouldn't be a very good time. I'll ask him when you might come over for a visit. Okay?"

"You promise you'll ask him?" Charlie insisted.

Justine hugged him tighter. "Of course I will. And I'll tell him hello for you."

Seemingly satisfied, Charlie slipped out of his mother's embrace and went back to the shrieking, gooing twins.

"What are you going to see Roy about?" Kitty asked, glancing from Charlie to Justine.

"Not what you're thinking," Justine answered, knowing her aunt was thinking about Charlie and whether she'd decided to tell Roy that he was his son. "Rose and I have found a peculiarity with the ranch finances, and we've both decided Roy needs to know about it.''

"Finances?" Chloe repeated sharply. "Roy Pardee doesn't need to know we're nearly broke! That has nothing to do with the twins."

"What finances are you talking about?" Kitty demanded.

"Rose will fill you both in while I'm gone."

Justine went on out the door, and was nearly to her pickup truck when Kitty caught up to her.

"Justine, are you sure you know what you're doing?"

"What do you mean?"

The older woman made a helpless gesture with her hands. "I mean about seeing Roy. Why not let Rose go talk to him?"

"Surprisingly, Rose does seem to trust Roy. But she doesn't know him like I do. I think— It would be better if I talked to him about this."

Kitty made a snorting noise. "A person doesn't have to know a sheriff personally to give him evidence, or whatever it is you think you've found."

"You believe I shouldn't see him. Is that it?"

Kitty placed a hand on Justine's arm. "I'm afraid you're going to keep on seeing him until the truth about Charlie finally slips out."

Justine opened the truck door and slid behind the wheel. "When I first told you that Roy was Charlie's father, you thought the man ought to know. Now you're worried he's going to somehow learn the truth. I don't understand you, Aunt Kitty."

"Well, I do think Roy ought to know about his son," Kitty reasoned. "But after you told me about him not wanting to...well, have a relationship with you, I guess I did get worried. Roy is a powerful man. He's bosom buddies with the district judge. He might just get it in his head to take Charlie away from you."

"No!" Justine shook her head emphatically. "Roy might be a hard man in many ways, but he'd never do that."

"Can you be so sure?"

"Roy told me he'd never do anything to hurt Charlie. And I think he knows what it would do to any child to tear it away from its mother."

Kitty's face remained puckered with worry. "I hope you're right, honey. Otherwise, you might find yourself in a fight with Roy that would make the Lincoln County range wars look like mild squabbles in comparison."

Justine reached for the ignition, then paused as she looked out at the falling dusk. "I've been thinking, Aunt Kitty. About Charlie and Roy and myself."

Kitty edged closer to the open door of the truck. "I know you've been in some sort of mental agony all this week, and I figured it had to be Roy. Nothing but a man can put such a look of torment on a woman's face."

Justine turned compassionate eyes on her aunt. It was no secret to any of the family that Kitty had once loved a married man. When he decided to stay with his wife, her aunt had blamed herself and sworn off men forever. That had been thirty years ago, and she was still living without a partner.

"I know you never got over the affair you had with Jim. But you didn't have a child to consider, Aunt Kitty."

"Thank God I didn't," the older woman said, then added in a wistful voice, "but sometimes, when a streak of loneliness hits me and I get to feeling a little selfish, I wish I had become pregnant back then. At least I would have had a child, something of my very own."

Justine could understand her aunt's feelings. As for herself, she wouldn't have been able to stand these past six years if Charlie hadn't given her a meaning and purpose in life.

Aunt and niece were silent for long moments. Finally

Justine said, "I'm beginning to think I have no choice but to tell Roy about Charlie."

Kitty gasped. "Tell him! Just like that?"

"Yes. He may not want me in his life, but I can't punish him or Charlie for that. I think Roy would love our son. And there's no doubt that Charlie needs him."

"But if Roy doesn't want to marry you—you might find another man. Someone who will want to make a family with you. And then what? It would be better if Roy wasn't in the picture."

Justine sighed. "But Roy is in the picture, Aunt Kitty. He's the father of my child. That will never change. Besides, if I can't have Roy, I don't want any man in my life."

"You're talking crazy now," Kitty said with a snort.

"Am I? You've lived thirty years without a man. I can, too." She started the engine and closed the door.

Kitty stepped back from the truck, but continued to study Justine through the open window. "I don't want you to be like me, honey. I want you to have someone to love you."

"My son loves me. But even that might change when he grows up and discovers I kept him from his father." She pulled the truck into gear. "I've got to go. Please put Charlie to bed for me. I'll try not to be gone long."

Justine drove away before Kitty could say more, but the older woman's words kept going around in her head as she drove the several miles to the Pardee Ranch.

Could she trust Roy not to take Charlie away from her? Or would he be so angry at her for keeping the fact of their son's conception from him that he'd use his law connections to spite her?

Dear God, she didn't know anymore. She only knew she had to come to some sort of decision or she was going to have a mental breakdown.

This past week at work, she'd simply gone through the motions of her job. At home, she was quiet and lethargic.

The only things that gave her any sort of enjoyment were Charlie and the twins. But she didn't know what to do about her state of mind.

She loved Roy. She desperately wanted to be with him. Yet he didn't want her, and nothing had ever hurt her so badly. Even six years ago, when he married Marla, her heart had somehow understood that he'd done it out of responsibility and not out of love. But this wall standing between them now was of his own choosing. He didn't want her company or her love. He simply didn't trust her.

The sky had grown nearly dark by the time Justine pulled up in front of Roy's house. Levi was quick to greet her as she stepped down from the truck, but Roy was nowhere in sight.

Seeing no lights on in the house, she waited for only a few moments, then started walking in the direction of the barn. More than likely he was still doing the evening chores.

Halfway there, she saw him riding the bay gelding up from the pasture. He lifted a hand to let her know he'd spotted her. Justine waved back and continued on to the barn to meet him.

Standing in the big doorway of the building, she waited for him to dismount from the horse.

"There's a light switch just to your left," he said. "Would you mind flipping it on?"

She reached to her left and found a switch attached to a two-by-four stud. She pushed it up, and a single dim bulb hanging from a rafter flared to life.

Roy led the gelding over to the tack room. Justine followed more slowly.

"Been checking on the cattle?" she asked.

Without glancing her way, he unbuckled the back cinch on the saddle. "I hadn't checked on the water tank since you and Charlie rode with me. I decided I'd better take a look this evening."

Just thinking about the day she and Charlie had spent with him was like a lance in her heart. She'd been filled with such hope that day. Now that hope was all but gone.

"We've had several showers since then," Justine said. "Rose and Chloe say our pastures are really green right now."

"Yeah," he said bluntly. "The ranches and orchards have been lucky so far this summer."

Justine unconsciously smoothed her hands down her hips. "I guess you're wondering why I'm here."

He continued to unsaddle the bay. "I'm sure you have a reason. You always seem to."

The awkwardness she'd first felt when he walked into the barn suddenly fled, and anger flared through her veins. "Well, if you're worried I'm here to seduce you, let me put your mind at ease. I didn't come over this evening for your body."

That brought his eyes around to her, and to Justine's surprise, a grin spread across his face. "I must be losing my sex appeal."

That would be impossible, she thought. Even when he was sixty years old, he would be a sexy man. And she figured he knew that.

"Don't worry, I'm sure you'll get it back. Probably tomorrow, when some woman sees you strutting down the street."

"I don't strut."

No, he didn't need to. He simply had to look at a woman with those steel-blue eyes to melt her bones.

She stepped closer. "Actually, I'm not sure if I have a good reason to be here tonight," she confessed. "You'll have to be the judge of that."

He looked at her with wry curiosity. Justine quickly waved him back to his task of unsaddling the bay. "Go ahead. I'll show you when you've finished."

Roy slipped the saddle from the horse's back, then carried it into the tack room. After he led the bay to his stall, gave him a bucket of grain and fresh water, he rejoined Justine at the doorway of the barn.

"Do you want to go up to the house?"

Justine shrugged. "Suit yourself."

"Let's go. I haven't eaten supper yet."

He turned off the light, then took her by the upper arm. They walked to the house in silence. Along the way, Justine was acutely aware of his warm fingers pressing into her flesh, the male scent of him, mixed with horse sweat, and the faint jingle of spurs on his boots.

Tomas, her daddy, had told her a long time ago that a wolf could never really be tamed or coaxed into trusting someone enough to let himself be loved. That was what Roy was, she realized, a lone wolf, who preferred to keep his heart to himself.

Inside the house, Roy put on a fresh pot of coffee. Justine waited by the cabinet counter until he was finished, then handed him the envelope of checks.

"Rose discovered these today, while she was doing some book work. Neither of us know what they might mean."

He glanced at her as he took the envelope. "You really did have something to show me."

She frowned at the surprise on his face. "What did you think? That I *was* here for your body?"

He sighed, his eyes soft on her face. "I never know about you, Justine. You're very unpredictable."

"I thought a man liked that in a woman."

He liked everything about her. He always had. Except for the fact that she'd left him and had some other man's child.

"Sit down. I'm going to heat a can of tamales. Want some?"

"No, thank you. I've already eaten this evening. But I will take a cup of coffee when it's ready."

She pulled out a chair at the kitchen table and motioned

for him to take a seat. "You sit down and look at what's inside that envelope while I heat the tamales."

He did as she suggested, and Justine busied herself finding the tamales and a saucepan to put them in. Once she had the food heating, she set a plate, silverware, a napkin and a coffee cup in front of him.

Roy quickly sifted through the checks. "You don't have any idea what these might have been written for? Or who they were written to?"

The urge to be near him pulled at Justine, and she lingered by his shoulder. He'd taken his hat off when they entered the house, and now her eyes drifted over the sandy waves of his hair. More than anything, she wanted to touch him. But she kept her hands firmly at her sides.

"No," she told him. "Rose carefully went through the ledger book, trying to match up the amount to a purchase of payment. She couldn't find anything. And believe me, Rose is good with numbers."

"Is this all of the checks?"

"We don't know. Rose is going to do some more digging tonight."

He placed the stack of documents on the table, then glanced up at Justine. "It appears to me as though your father was paying off a debt of some sort. Obviously one he didn't want his family to know about. Did you ever know of him keeping things about himself from you?"

Justine searched her mind. "Not really. There wasn't anything secretive about Daddy. He was a rancher who liked to raise cattle and racehorses." Shaking her head, she made a motion with her hand, indicating the stack of canceled checks. "Rose and I were wondering if the checks might have something to do with the twins. That's why I wanted you to see them."

He rubbed a hand over his jaws. "The idea seems remote. But we won't rule anything out until we find out who the money went to."

"Can you do that?"

He didn't find her question daunting. "Easy. We have the bank where the checks were deposited. And even though they were endorsed with Deposit Only, rather than a name, the account number on the back of the canceled checks tells us where that money went. I'll get a name."

Justine didn't know all about the laws of privacy or when a sheriff was permitted to break them, but she trusted Roy. He was the sheriff because he was good at it and because people trusted him.

She went over to the stove and stirred the tamales. Seeing the coffee had dripped, she carried the pot to the table and filled Roy's cup. "You know, I'm almost afraid to know what these checks are about. What if my father was into something illegal? It would kill my sisters."

"What about you?"

She passed a weary hand over her hair. "I wouldn't like it. But I know better than to put any man, even my father, on a pedestal. When a woman does that, she might as well get ready for a big disappointment."

She was referring to him, Roy thought. He'd disappointed her six years ago, and he supposed he was still failing to fulfil her hopes and dreams. At that moment, he knew what she'd been referring to when she talked about him living in a fog. Until now, he hadn't really thought of what their breakup might have done to her. He'd only been thinking of himself.

Justine checked on the tamales. They were steaming-hot, so she carried the pot to the table and scooped several onto Roy's plate.

Roy thanked her and picked up his fork. An hour ago, he'd been starving, and anxious to get back to the house and eat. Now he didn't care if he ate or not. All he could think about was Justine and how good it felt to have her here, moving around the kitchen, hovering over his shoulder.

He took a bite of the tamales. Justine sat down in the chair next to his.

"Have you gotten anywhere with the birth records?" she asked.

His eyes were drawn to her face, and the red waves surrounding it.

"Not yet. But we have a long ways to go." He swallowed the tamale and automatically took another bit. "How is Charlie?"

Her eyes dropped to her coffee cup. "He begged to come with me."

He couldn't tear his gaze away from her. "Why didn't you bring him?"

She sighed as the burden of her secret crushed down on her. "I really didn't figure you wanted to see me or Charlie. Besides, it was getting near his bedtime when I left the ranch." She glanced at her watch. "Actually, it's getting close to mine now."

Rising to her feet, Justine carried her coffee cup over to the cabinets, dumped what was left in the sink, then started to the door.

"I'd better be going," she told him. "You can let me know about the checks after you've had a chance to look into them."

Justine hadn't meant to leave this abruptly. But once he mentioned Charlie, she'd felt cornered and wounded. She'd come over here with the faint notion of letting him know that Charlie was his son. But now she realized she couldn't bring herself to do it. A part of her was afraid that what Kitty feared might really happen. Roy might want to hurt her so badly he would use any means to get Charlie.

Over at the table, Roy's eyes continued to cling to her, and suddenly he was struck by how much he wanted her to stay. All this week, he'd felt as if he were missing an arm or leg, or some other important part of him. Now that she was here, he felt whole again. Whole and happy.

Forgetting the meal, he rose from the table and went to her.

"Do you have to leave now?"

Wasn't that what he wanted? For her to keep her distance? Averting her eyes from his, she said, "I think I'd better. I've already imposed on you enough tonight."

She sounded so formal and polite. Not like a woman he'd once made love to. He knew he could blame himself for her distance. He'd more or less asked for it.

"I wanted to call you several times this week," he said in a low voice.

Her eyes fluttered up to his. "You *wanted* to call me?"

He nodded gravely. "I guess that's hard for you to believe."

She tried to laugh, but it came out more like a bitter sob. "It's not hard to believe. It's impossible."

He sighed. "You're not making this any easier for me."

Her delicate auburn brows arched innocently. "What are you talking about? I brought you a stack of evidence, or what might be evidence. Now I'm going home. I'm making it very easy for you."

His hand reached up and curled around her throat. It was warm and damp, and the beat of her heart throbbed against his palm. "I'm trying to tell you that I've missed you."

Her eyes fell to the toes of his boots. "I'm sure that galled you."

"I didn't like it," he agreed. "But I'm facing up to it. Admitting it to myself and to you. That's a start, isn't it?"

Did he really want a start? The question brought her gaze back up to his. "I don't want any man who doesn't want me. Can't you understand that, Roy?"

He mouthed a curse word under his breath. If he wanted her anymore he'd be stark raving crazy. "I do want you, Justine."

"But it irks you that you do. Is that supposed to make me happy?"

"Wanting you doesn't irk me, Justine, it scares the hell out of me."

The truth of what he was saying was in his eyes. She moved closer and lifted her hand to his face. Tracing the fine lines at the corner of one eye, she said, "I didn't think anything could scare you."

"Loving you does."

"I'm still not so sure you love me."

"Maybe it's time I showed you."

"No— Roy—" Her protest was blotted out by his lips, and she knew it was too late to run from him. Her heart was melting, her blood was singing through her veins.

With a groan of desire, she leaned into him, curled her arms around his waist.

Roy kissed her for a moment longer. Then, bending, he scooped her up in his arms and carried her out of the kitchen.

"What are you doing?" she whispered frantically as they moved through a darkened hallway.

"Sssh..." he said. "Don't talk. Talking isn't going to fix what ails us."

But she had to talk, she thought through a haze of desire. She had to tell him about Charlie. Before it was too late. Before he hated her.

He made a left turn with her and entered an open door. Seconds later, Justine felt a mattress against her back and Roy's body pressing down on hers.

Moonlight filtered through the slatted blinds on the window and illuminated the room enough for Justine to see his face hovering only inches above hers.

"This is my bed, Justine. It's where you belong. Where you've always belonged."

Hope dared to surge through her. "For one night? A few nights? Is that what you're saying?"

His head bent, and he pressed a kiss behind her ear. "I'm

saying you were right, Justine. It's time we started making the past up to each other.''

Her mind was suddenly reeling. He wanted a future with her! He was saying it with words, showing her with kisses. For years she had dreamed of this moment, and for just as long she'd told herself that a dream was all it could be. But now it was actually happening, and her senses were so shocked, she couldn't think or plan or know what to do. Except love him.

"Oh, Roy, are you sure? You've always said you didn't want a wife or family. You said you didn't trust me.''

With his hands on her face, he kissed the corners of her mouth, her nose and chin. "I'm tired of hanging on to the past, Justine. I'd rather hang on to you. And Charlie.''

And Charlie. Dear heaven, she had to tell him now! She had to explain and hope that he would understand and be happy to know that he was really Charlie's father.

With a desperate groan, she circled her arms around his neck and brought her lips against his.

It was all the response Roy needed. He crushed her to him, threaded his fingers through her long hair and explored the sweet, giving softness of her lips.

In moments, the need to be closer had become a necessity for Roy. With urgent hands, he tugged Justine's T-shirt over her head, then pulled the straps of her bra down her arms until the fabric pulled away from her breasts.

As his mouth nuzzled its way toward her rigid nipple, Justine felt herself fast losing her grip, and she realized she had to speak now. She wanted him to know about Charlie before they made love.

"Roy, there's something I need—'' Her hands slid across his shoulders and into the thick waves at the back of his head. "Something...I have to tell you.''

Resting his chin on her breast, he looked up at her. "If you're worried about protection, I've got it.''

Suddenly everything inside her was shaking with fear.

She loved Roy so much. If she lost him now, she didn't know how she could bear it. "No. I'm not worried about birth control. I want to explain about when I left six years ago."

He groaned with frustration. "I don't want to hear it, Justine. That's in the past. Done with. Tonight, we're starting over."

"But...you need to know that—"

His hands gently framed her face. "Answer me one thing, Justine. Do you love me?"

A little sob broke past her lips. "Oh, Roy, I love you with all my heart. I always have. I always will."

A smile curved the corners of his mouth, and his blue eyes glittered with longing. "Then that's all I need to know."

"But, Roy—"

Before she could go any farther, the telephone at the head of the bed rang. Roy lifted his head and stared at the intrusive instrument.

"I don't want to answer it."

Justine didn't want him to answer it, either. She didn't want this moment between them to be broken. But he was the sheriff, and if he was needed, she couldn't, in all good conscience, keep him to herself.

"You'd better answer it, Roy. It might be important."

He hesitated, and the ringing continued. Justine knew the sound was mentally pulling him away from her.

"You're important, Justine. As important to me as my job."

"I'm not going anywhere," she assured him. "We have tomorrow, and all our tomorrows, to look forward to now."

With one fluid movement, he rolled away from her and snatched up the receiver.

"Sheriff Pardee here."

Justine turned onto her side so that she could watch him.

As soon as he began to listen to the caller on the end of the line, a scowl wrinkled his face.

"When did this happen? Okay. I'll be there in a few minutes."

He hung up the phone, then looked regretfully at Justine. "I guess it's obvious I have to go."

Scooting up in the bed, she reached for her T-shirt. "What's happened now? You don't have to go track down some crazy killer, do you?"

"It's nothing like that," he assured her.

"Roy, when you go out like this, it scares me. I can't help but worry that something might happen to you."

Shaking his head, he leaned toward her and ran his hand tenderly over her bare shoulder. It touched Roy's heart to know that she cared that much about him, but worrying about him was the last thing he wanted her to do.

"Justine, honey, this is nothing for you to worry about. It's not anything dangerous. One of my deputies caught a big fish tonight. I've got to go question him. Or at least try to question him before his lawyer gets there and shuts him up."

"A big fish?"

"Just one of many in a drug circle."

So there wasn't any chance he could put this interruption off until tomorrow, Justine thought. She straightened her bra and quickly tugged the T-shirt back over her head. Then, scooting to the edge of the bed, she searched for her loafers.

Roy picked them up from where they'd fallen from her feet and handed them to her. "It might be hours before I get back. I don't suppose you could wait for me?"

She wanted desperately to say yes. She didn't want this night to end. Especially without him knowing about Charlie. But now that he had to leave, there wasn't any way she could spring that sort of news on him. She was going to have to postpone telling him for the time being.

Rising to her feet, she slid her arms around his waist. "I want to, Roy. But Charlie wouldn't understand why his mother wasn't home in the morning. It might even frighten him."

He nodded with understanding. "I know you're right. And I wouldn't want the little guy to be upset. But I hate like hell to leave you now," he added in a husky voice.

She raised up on tiptoe and kissed his lips. "I'll meet you tomorrow after work."

His hands lingered in her hair as he held her close. "I love you, Justine. Just saying it makes me feel like a different man."

But how much did he love her? Would he still feel the same way tomorrow, when she told him about Charlie? It terrified her to even think about it now.

"You don't know how happy it makes me to hear you say it," she told him.

His arm around her shoulders, he guided Justine out of the room and down the dark hallway to the kitchen. The plate of tamales sat uneaten on the table, and she realized he was going to go back to work hungry.

"You didn't get to eat. Would you like for me to make you a sandwich to take with you?"

Roy smiled at her concern for him. "No. One of the deputies will go out and get fast food for me."

"I'll clean up this mess before I leave," she told him as she followed him to the door.

Grabbing her by the chin, he placed a rough kiss on her mouth. "I'm not worried about the mess. I'm worried about making it through tomorrow, until I can see you again."

"Call me," she urged.

He stepped out the door. "I promise," he said, then hurried down the deck and into the dark yard.

Moments later, Justine heard his Bronco fire to life, then the sound of the vehicle pulling away.

On weak knees, she walked over to the table, but before

she could reach for the plate of tamales, her eyes blurred with tears and a painful sob rose up in her throat.

Roy loved her. He'd finally decided he could trust her. And now she had to tell him she'd kept Charlie's conception a secret from him for six long years. She couldn't imagine what that was going to do to him. Or to her and Charlie.

Chapter Nine

Early the next morning, Roy was sipping his coffee and eyeing the stack of checks lying on his desk.

"That's right, Grady," he said to the lawman on the other end of the phone line. "I have the name of the bank and the account number of the depositor. How long will it take you to get me a name? That soon? Good. I'm sending a deputy down there now. He should get there in a couple of hours. If my hunch is right, this name is going to pay off in a case I'm working on. Yeah. Thanks, Grady."

Roy hung up the phone. Then, leaning his head over his desk and toward the door, he yelled, "Randall, get in here!"

The tall, lanky deputy quickly came into Roy's office. "Yes, sir?"

"I want you to drive to Las Cruces and do a little footwork."

"Now?"

"That's right. I want you to get down there and start searching through the birth records. I've already contacted the authorities, so they'll be ready for you."

The young deputy took off his hat and scratched his head. "This is still that thing about the twins? Boy, Sheriff Pardee, I don't see how sifting through all those computer records is gonna help. For all we know, those twins might have been born back in New York."

"If that turns out to be a possibility, then I'll send you to New York to search, Randall. But right now, I've got a hunch they were born in Las Cruces. When you get there, the sheriff is going to give you a name. It's the name I think will be on the birth certificate."

"You sound pretty confident."

"I am. Now get going."

Randall plopped his hat back on his head. "How long am I supposed to stay?"

"Till you get the job done."

The young man's mouth fell open. "But that might take days!"

"Then you'll be in Las Cruces for days," Roy told him. "So get out of here, before I decide to send Billy."

Not liking the sound of his boss's threat, Randall hurried out of the room.

"And Randall," Roy yelled after him, "call me the second you find anything!"

"Yes, sir!"

With Randall finally out of sight, Roy picked up the checks Justine had given him and leaned back in his chair.

Tomas Murdock. The rancher's name was signed on each document in bold black strokes. Each time Roy looked at the signature, he got a bad feeling.

For Justine's sake, he hoped his suspicions were wrong. As far as he knew, she had always been very close to her father. He didn't relish the idea of telling her that the man she'd loved and respected wasn't all she believed him to be.

Later that afternoon, Roy was trying to get his mind off

Justine and get something done on a stack of paperwork when the phone on his desk rang.

He picked it up, hoping it was her, and was mildly surprised to hear his deputy's voice on the other end.

"Randall? What's the matter? Did the car break down?"

"Oh, no, Sheriff Pardee. I made it down here this morning just fine. I'm callin' 'cause I think I've found the information you wanted."

If Randall had found the identity of the twins' parents, he was going to give him a bonus out of his own pocket.

"Let me have it, and we'll see," Roy told him.

"I've got it here in front of me. And you know what, Roy, you were right about that name the sheriff gave me."

"It was a woman?"

"Yes, sir. Belinda Waller. Turns out she's the mother of the babies."

"Are you sure, Randall? If this is just speculation, we can't use it. You know that, don't you?"

"It's not speculation, Sheriff Pardee. I've got the computer screen right here in front of me. And it's pretty damn obvious I've found the parents. The other name on those checks is the father."

"Tomas Murdock is listed as the father?"

"Yep. Belinda Waller, mother. Tomas Murdock, father. They were born nearly six months ago, here in a Las Cruces hospital."

Roy let out a heavy sigh. He'd suspected the old man had had something to do with the twins, but not to this extent. He couldn't imagine how Justine and her family were going to react to hearing they had a new brother and sister.

"Randall, you've done good. Get a copy of the birth certificates and get back up here with it. Did Grady have any information on the woman? Is she still in Las Cruces?"

"No, sir. She didn't have any sort of criminal record. But she's split from the last known address she had here."

"Well, we'll find her. We've got something to go on now."

"Uh, Sheriff Pardee, there's something else I wanted to ask you. Do you have any relatives down here in Las Cruces?"

"Me? No, I don't have many relatives, period. Why?" Roy asked with wry amusement. "Did you find a Pardee listed among the felons?"

Randall awkwardly cleared his throat. "No. When I was scrolling through the birth records, I found a Roy Pardee."

"Well, I wasn't born in Las Cruces, Randall. I was born in Ruidoso."

"No. This isn't *your* birth record, Sheriff Pardee. This is—well, it's kinda strange, sir."

His curiosity piqued now, Roy raised up in his chair. "Spit it out, Randall. I haven't got all day, and neither have you."

"Let me find it," Randall told his boss as he quickly scrolled back through the records. "Okay, here it is. Roy Pardee is listed as father. The birth was a little over five years ago."

Five years ago. A sick feeling suddenly rushed through Roy. "What's the mother's name?"

"That's just it, Sheriff Pardee. It's the same as the twins' daddy. Murdock. Justine Murdock."

Roy felt as if someone had whacked him in the midsection with an ax. He couldn't breathe or think. He was numb with shock.

Several moments passed in silence as Randall waited for his boss to make a reply. When the line continued to remain silent, he decided to yell.

"Sheriff Pardee! Roy! Are you still there? Are you listening to me?"

Roy forced himself to take a deep breath, and then another. "Yeah," he finally answered, "I'm still here."

"I hope I haven't opened a can of worms here, sir. I was just searching for evidence, not—anything else."

"Don't worry about it, Randall."

"But if someone has wrongly named you the father of their child, well, I thought you'd want to know about it."

"What is the child's name, Randall?" he asked, his lips so stiff and cold he could hardly form the words.

The deputy read, "'Charles Tomas.' He weighed seven pounds and twelve ounces and was twenty-one inches long."

Any other time, those facts and figures would have simply been information to Roy. But this was *his* son. He should have been privy to all these things the day Charlie was born!

"I haven't been wrongly accused, Randall. Charlie is my son."

"Oh—I didn't know."

Neither had he, Roy wanted to yell. Instead, he kept his voice flat as he slowly said, "It looks as though you've done all you can do down there for right now, Randall. Come on home, and I'll see you when you get back."

"Right, Sheriff Pardee. And, sir, you don't have to worry about me, uh...mentioning this to anyone."

Anger had driven the numbing shock from Roy's body. It was shaking his hands, throbbing his temples.

"It doesn't matter if you do, Randall. 'Cause I sure as hell intend to!"

Justine dashed a brush through her red waves, then hurried down the hallway to the front desk. Of all the days for her to have to work past five, she thought, this had to be the one.

"Carlita, do I have any phone messages?"

The woman glanced over to the scratch pad she kept by the telephone. "Only one. Your aunt said she was going to her friend's for supper, and that Charlie would be with Chloe and Rose.''

Justine nodded. ''Is that all? Sheriff Pardee hasn't called?''

Carlita shook her head. ''No. There hasn't been any other calls for you.''

Justine reached for the phone and punched in the number of the sheriff's department in Carrizozo. She figured Roy would have already called to tell her where to meet him this evening. Perhaps he'd had to go out on an emergency.

The dispatcher quickly informed her that the sheriff had left the office this afternoon and hadn't been back since. ''Is this an emergency?'' she asked Justine.

''No. I—just needed to contact him. Thank you anyway.''

''You might try his home,'' the woman suggested.

Justine couldn't imagine that Roy had driven all the way to the Pardee Ranch, when he'd been planning to meet her after work, but she would try the number, just in case something had called him home.

''Yes. I will. Thank you.''

''Problems?'' Carlita asked as Justine pressed the receiver button.

Justine smiled—something she'd been doing all day long. ''Don't ever get involved with a lawman, Carlita. You can never find them when you want them.''

Carlita let out a saucy laugh. ''If I had a man like Sheriff Pardee, I'd be in big trouble, 'cause I'd be looking for him all the time.''

Waving away Carlita's teasing, she punched in the number at Roy's ranch. It rang several times before Justine decided to hang up. ''Oh, well,'' she said with a shrug, ''it looks as though I've been stood up.''

''I wouldn't worry, honey. I'm sure the man has a good reason.''

Justine told Carlita goodbye for the evening and left the

clinic. She wasn't really sure what to do next. She hated to drive home and have Roy miss her here. Maybe if she waited in the parking lot for a few minutes, he'd show up.

She sat in her truck for thirty minutes, watching for the approach of his Bronco. After a while, both Carlita and Dr. Bellamy left the building and, except for her, the parking lot was empty.

Feeling more than a little deflated, Justine decided to drive on home. Once she reached Ruidoso Downs, she made a quick pass by the police station, but there was no sign of Roy's Bronco, or any vehicle connected to the Lincoln County Sheriff's Department, parked outside the building.

Justine didn't know what to think. Roy had promised to call and meet her after work. He'd seemed so anxious and eager about it. Yet he'd done neither. She couldn't imagine what might have happened. As for her, all day long she had been counting the minutes until she could see him again. She'd expected him to be counting the minutes, too.

Justine had driven only a few miles toward Hondo when an ominous feeling began to settle over her. She told herself to shake it, but the more she tried to pass it off, the more worried she became. These past few weeks, she'd come to realize just how dangerous Roy's job could be at times. He was a target for all sorts of deranged people.

Her family wasn't expecting her home until later tonight. To ease her mind, she would drive over to the Pardee Ranch and see for herself if Roy was there.

More than thirty minutes later, she pulled to a stop outside Roy's log house and was warily surprised to see his Bronco parked in the shade of a cottonwood tree.

What was he doing home? Had something happened to one of the cows? The horses?

Climbing down from her truck, she glanced toward the barn. At the same time, Levi bounded up to greet her.

"Hello, boy," she said to the dog as she gave him a loving pat on the head. "Where's your master?"

With a wag of his tail, the dog urged her around to the back of the house and up on the deck. "I'm going to see if you're as smart as Rin Tin Tin," she said to Levi as she knocked on the door.

After a moment, footsteps sounded through the house. She shot the scruffy dog an impressive look. "I guess you are. You probably belong in the movies."

"What are you doing here?"

Justine's head jerked up, and she saw Roy standing behind the screen door. "What do you mean, what am I doing here?" she asked with a little laugh. "You were supposed to meet me in town!"

"So I was," he said in a clipped voice.

His sudden switch from hot to cold completely baffled Justine. She stared at him, wondering and waiting for him to explain.

When he didn't make any sort of reply, she asked, "Have you been drinking?"

He snorted. "If I were a drinking man, Justine, I would have already been stone drunk."

He turned away from the screen and out of her sight. Not waiting for an invitation, Justine opened the door and stepped into the kitchen.

Roy was nowhere to be seen, so she walked down the hallway to the living room. The house was closed and stuffy. She didn't know why he hadn't opened the windows or turned on the air conditioner. Did he not feel the heat?

Justine found him standing in front of a picture window, his hard profile staring out at the desert hills surrounding the ranch house. She walked over to him.

"Is something wrong, Roy?" She knew the question sounded inane, but what else could she ask? Last night, when she left him, he'd been happy, loving, eager for them to put the past behind them.

He let out a caustic laugh. "Oh, I wouldn't call it wrong," he finally said in a sneering voice. "Actually, I guess you could say everything is all right now. I've made a narrow escape."

She wanted to reach out to him, but the look on his face warned her that he would only shake away her touch. "You had— Did something happen at work?"

He smiled coldly. "Did something happen at work? Sit down, sweet Justine, and I'll tell you all about it." He made a sweeping gesture with his arm toward the couch. "In fact, before you drove up, I was just sitting here trying to figure out the best way to give you the news."

"News? You've heard something about the twins?"

He pointed toward the couch. "I said, sit down."

She glared at him. "Don't order me about, Roy. I'm not one of your deputies. And I'm not in the mood to play games. So if you've got something to tell me, get on with it."

His smile still cruel and goading, he reached down and patted her cheek. "What's the hurry, honey? After all, time doesn't mean anything to you. Five years. Six years. The way you figure things, that doesn't mean anything to a man's life."

Her heart pounding with both dread and anger, she slapped his hand away from her face. "You have been drinking!"

His blue eyes were suddenly twin glaciers. "Hellfire, Justine, I've never drunk alcohol, and you know it! But I do think we need a drink, all right. A toast of celebration." He turned and motioned for her to follow him back to the kitchen.

Furious, Justine ran after him and grabbed his arm. "Damn it, Roy, I don't want a drink. I want you to tell me what's going on!"

He caught her by the hand and tugged her roughly down

the hallway. By the time they reached the kitchen, Justine was flushed and longing to kick him in the shins.

"It's hot in here," she told him. "Why haven't you opened the windows, or turned on the air conditioner?"

"I haven't had time. I've been too busy thinking about you. But don't let the heat get you down, honey, 'cause it's about to get hotter. Ready to do a little sweating?"

Jerking loose of him, she went over to the kitchen sink and shoved up the window, then pushed up two more that faced out toward the deck.

Roy opened the refrigerator and scanned the almost bare shelves. "Looks like it has to be orange juice or apple cider. Which do you want?"

"Neither," she snapped. "I'm not thirsty."

He made a tsking noise with his tongue. "Now, Justine, don't be unsociable. We're going to have a toast."

"A toast to what?" she asked as he took two glasses down from the cabinet.

He was like some sort of mad scientist, she thought wildly. One who had brewed a strange concoction, drunk it and turned into a total stranger.

"Why, we're going to drink to three births, that's what."

Her brows arched as she watched him fill the glasses with cider. The thought of taking one sip nearly made her vomit.

"Births? What births?"

Roy's blue eyes glittered strangely as he carried the glass of cider to her and pressed it in her hand.

"The three Murdock births. It's a joyous occasion, so let's drink up. This is Hondo Valley's finest cider. I just bought it a few days ago."

He swallowed some of the apple drink. Her mind whirling with his strange innuendos, Justine simply stared at him.

"I don't know of any Murdock births," she said flatly.

"Oh, that's right," he drawled. "I forgot to give you the

news. The twins… Cute little Adam and Anna aren't just two babies that were dumped on the Bar M from out of the blue. They're your brother and sister.''

Justine felt as if he'd kicked her in the stomach. She tried to take a breath, but nothing seemed to fill her lungs.

The room began to sway, and she made a frantic grab for the cabinet counter behind her.

''You…aren't serious. The twins can't be my brother and sister!''

He shot her a look of feigned innocence. ''Why can't they be?''

''Daddy is dead.''

His face grim now, Roy nodded. ''Yes. He is. But count back, Justine. Your father was alive and well when the twins were conceived. He was still alive when they were born.''

Justine forced herself to mentally calculate how long it would take to get the twins to six months of age. Roy was right, she realized, as the time span fell into place. But it didn't make sense. How could it be? Her mother would have still been alive when the babies were conceived. Her father… She shuddered as her mind refused to accept the fact of his betrayal and deceit.

''Where did you hear such a thing? Has someone in town been gossiping to your deputies?''

His mouth twisted into a sneer. ''A sheriff doesn't put stock in gossip, Justine, he has to deal with hard, cold facts. And I've got them. I've got the birth certificate to prove everything.''

He was telling the truth. She could see it on his face. But what he was saying was so shocking, so unbelievable, she simply couldn't fathom it.

''But the mother—that woman. Who is she? Why did she leave the twins?''

His eyes ran over her pale face, and for a moment Roy felt ashamed of himself for throwing the truth so bluntly in her face. "Her name is Belinda Waller. She was living in Las Cruces at the time of the twins' birth. That's where your father's checks were going. To her. But whether it was money to keep her quiet or to support her, we won't have any idea until we find her."

The twins, Adam and Anna, were her half brother and sister, she thought dazedly. She couldn't believe it and yet somehow it seemed right. The two babies had fit in with the family as if they truly belonged there. And now she knew why. They were Murdocks. Just like she and Rose and Chloe.

Her eyes lifted to his. "You said something about three births. Was there actually a set of triplets?"

What little compassion Roy had felt for her a second ago dissolved under a fresh rush of outrage.

"No," he said tightly. "The third birth has nothing to do with the twins. This was a separate birth certificate. Charles Tomas Murdock. Born September twenty-fourth. Seven pounds and twelve ounces. Twenty-one inches long. Mother, Justine Murdock." He took a step toward her, and was glad to see the last bit of color drain from her face. "Father, Roy Pardee."

So he finally knew. It was all over, she thought as a lead weight hit the pit of her stomach. Or was it only the beginning?

She met the hard, accusing glare of his eyes. "How did you find out?"

"I have a very observant deputy on the case of the twins. While he was searching through the birth records in Las Cruces, he stumbled onto his boss's name. The rest, as they say, is…history."

"I was trying to tell you last night. You wouldn't let me."

He held up his hand. "Don't—don't even say it. Last night, a week ago. A month ago. What the hell difference would that have made?"

She suddenly felt so cold she was outwardly shivering. But how could that be, when the night was so hot and this house so stifling?

"You're right. It wouldn't make any difference," she said through gritted teeth. "I carried Charlie in my womb for nine months alone. I went through eighteen long, excruciating hours of labor alone. I nursed him through his colic months, through his teething and temperatures, alone. When he woke in the night, crying and afraid, I comforted him alone. Because you weren't there. You weren't there through any of it. So don't try to act hurt with me, Roy Pardee. You don't know what *hurt* is."

His whole face had turned to stone. "I wasn't there because you chose not to tell me about Charlie. You deliberately kept him from me!"

She was still gripping the glass of cider with one hand and the cabinet counter with the other. But in her mind's eye she was lunging at him, beating her fist against his chest. "You made your choice, Roy. You chose to marry Marla. She came first with you."

"I thought she was pregnant with my child!"

"I *was* pregnant with your child, Roy. I gave birth to your son. Not Marla."

"Why didn't you tell me?"

"And have you marry me out of obligation? No thanks. You didn't want a family then. And I was a fool for thinking you wanted one now!"

He stepped closer, but stopped himself from touching her. "I did want one. But just when I thought I could trust you, I find out you lied to me. You've been lying for six years!"

Suddenly she wanted to hurt him. She wanted him to feel the same pain she'd felt that day she left for Las Cruces, carrying their child inside her and knowing she could never tell him.

Her insides clawing with rage, she flung the glass of

cider straight into his face. The sweet liquid drenched his hair and shirt and dripped from his chin.

"You're not the victim here, Roy. Charlie is. And until you can see that, I don't want you around him!"

He wiped his face roughly against his shirtsleeve, then stared at her coldly. "Get out!"

"Gladly."

Justine walked stiffly out of the house and down the steps of the deck. Levi met her on the ground and escorted her around to her pickup.

Too numb and shaky to even open the truck door, she sat down on the running board and stared up at the darkening sky. "I feel sorry for you, Levi," she told the dog, who'd nudged his way between her knees. "Your master is a hard, selfish man."

Levi let out a soulful whine. Justine bent forward and hugged the dog's neck. "I know, old boy," she said through tear-blurred eyes. "You love him as much as I do."

Chapter Ten

When Roy came upon the scene, he saw that the woman was hysterical. Her Spanish came out in rapid-fire spurts, between racking wails and sobs.

Randall was trying his best to calm her, but his knowledge of the language was limited, and he couldn't pick up half of what she was trying to tell him.

Shouldering the deputy aside, Roy took the woman by the arm and spoke to her in a low, firm voice.

Seeing that he was the sheriff calmed her somewhat. She wiped tears from her eyes and began to explain to him that her son, Jorge, had been missing for more than an hour now. Or at least she believed it had been that long. He was seven years old. He'd been wearing blue jeans and boots and a yellow tank top. Nothing more.

"When did you realize your son was missing?" he asked her.

She pointed frantically toward the orchard behind the back of the small house. "I came out to call him in to lunch. He'd been playing under the apple trees. But he was gone. I searched everywhere for him. Even in the house."

"Was your son angry with you about something? Has he ever threatened to run away from home?"

She shook her head, then suddenly paused. "He'd been crying this morning because he wanted to see his daddy. Tomorrow is the Fourth of July, and my husband always shoots firecrackers for Jorge."

"Where is your husband?"

"In Alto. We're separated now."

"You think your son might be trying to get to his father?"

She shrugged, then sniffed as a fresh spate of tears rolled from her eyes. "I don't know, but he has often threatened to walk there. I told him it is more than thirty miles to Alto from here. But he doesn't understand miles. He only wants to be with his daddy."

Roy patted the woman's shoulder. "Don't worry, Ms. Sanchez, we'll find Jorge for you. Do you have a dog? Would it have followed your son?"

She nodded vigorously and described the dog. Roy left her and motioned for Randall. "Call Mike and have him bring the hounds. The boy is on foot around here somewhere. Apparently he's got it into his head to walk to Alto to find his father."

"Poor little tyke," Randall said sadly. "When parents decide to live apart, they don't stop to think how they make their children suffer."

As Randall walked away, Roy thought about the harsh reality of his deputy's words. Was he hurting Charlie the same way little Jorge's father was hurting his son? Dear God, he didn't want to think so!

You're not the victim here. Charlie is. And until you can see that, I don't want you around him!

Justine's words struck him like a bolt of lightning. And for the first time in the two weeks since he'd discovered Charlie was his son, Roy could see past his own anger and pain. He could see what he really wanted, for his son, for himself, and for Justine.

"Justine, you know you're going to have to see the man again," Kitty said as she took a long sip of iced tea.

Justine pushed at the food on her plate. Kitty and Rose had gone to great pains to make homemade enchiladas just for her. She appreciated their thoughtfulness in trying to cheer her up, but she couldn't help remembering the last time she'd eaten the Mexican dish. It had been with Roy, the night she told him she still loved him. He hadn't wanted to hear her feelings for him then any more than he wanted to hear that Charlie was his son, she thought sadly.

"I'm not going to see Roy for any reason." Since Charlie had already eaten and gone outside to the courtyard to play, she didn't bother to hide the bitterness in her voice.

Several days ago, she'd told her son that Roy was his daddy. The child had been ecstatic over the news. And even though Roy hadn't come to see him, Charlie was still devotedly loyal to the man, certain that he would show up sooner or later.

"But what about the twins' mother?" Rose asked. "We've got to find out about her. And Roy is the only person who can do that for us."

Justine put down her fork and reached for her tea glass. "Don't worry. Roy is a sheriff, first and foremost. If he finds out anything about Belinda Waller, he'll let us know."

"I'm not so sure about that," Chloe said from across the table. "He may keep the information to himself, just to spite Justine for keeping the facts about Charlie from him."

"Chloe!" Kitty scolded. "You know the circumstances about Charlie's birth, and why your sister did what she did. It's not your place to blame her!"

Shaking her head, Chloe shot Justine an apologetic look. "I'm not blaming Justine for anything. I'm simply saying that since Roy hasn't shown his face around here in the past two weeks, it's pretty obvious he's damn angry at Justine.''

"I'm not exactly happy with him, either," Justine muttered.

Rose quietly placed her napkin on her dirty plate. "This is ridiculous," she said to the other three women. "None of this is going to help matters one iota. When Justine discovered she was pregnant and she thought Marla was, too, she did what she thought was best and took herself out of the picture. And Roy, not knowing about Justine or Marla's deception, did what he thought was best. Neither one of them can be blamed. It was all just a bad set of circumstances.''

"Well, I don't know about you three," Chloe shot back, "but I'd like to hunt Marla down and wring her scrawny little neck. Wouldn't you, Justine?"

"I don't have any desire to hunt down Marla and exact revenge on her. She got her punishment when Roy divorced her," Justine told her sister.

"You're bigger-hearted than I am, sis," Chloe replied.

Kitty suddenly dabbed at her eyes. "Well, putting Roy and Justine aside, I'm still brokenhearted over what your daddy did to my sister Lola. He's the one I'd like to choke. I just wish he was still alive so I could do it!"

Coming to terms with the idea of Tomas Murdock having an affair while their mother had been an invalid had been hard for the entire family to accept. The only good thing any of them could find in the whole ugly mess was the fact that the twins were their blood relatives. Everyone, including Kitty, was thrilled about that.

"Daddy was a man, Aunt Kitty." Justine spoke with weary certainty. "And I've never seen any man who didn't put his own selfish needs before anyone else."

Rising to her feet, Justine began to unbuckle Adam and

Anna from their high chairs. "I'm going to take the babies for a walk in their stroller."

A few minutes later, in the extra bedroom the women had turned into a nursery, Justine changed the twins' diapers, then smoothed sunscreen over their exposed skin.

She'd just finished slathering Adam's arms when Rose entered the room.

"Need some help?" she asked Justine.

"Thanks, but I think I have them just about ready to go outside."

Rose watched Justine gently place their half brother in a nearby playpen. "I believe you're as crazy about these two babies as Chloe and I are," she said.

"Of course I am. Why wouldn't I be?"

Rose shrugged. "Well, it's different with you. You have Charlie. Chloe and I will probably...never have children of our own."

"I wouldn't say that, Rose. Chloe can always adopt, and in your case, you're still a healthy young woman. You might eventually meet a man and have a child of your own."

A forlorn shadow passed over Rose's face. "Chloe has her sights set on keeping the twins. As for me, having some man's baby...well, that just isn't going to happen."

Justine didn't know what else to say to her sister. Rose believed the worst of herself and every man who got within speaking distance of her. She didn't know what it was going to take to bring her older sister out of her hiding place.

Walking over to the baby crib sitting in one corner of the room, Rose trailed a loving finger over the wooden railings. "I really think you ought to go to Roy, Justine. He's Charlie's father, and whether you want to admit it or not, you need him."

Rose's suggestion took Justine by surprise, and she walked over to her sister. "Rose, you of all people know how it feels to be rejected by a man. I can't imagine you wanting me to go over there and give him the chance to tear me up again.''

Rose gave Justine's shoulder a squeeze. ''You aren't happy like you are. And I doubt very much that Roy is, either.''

No, Justine had to admit, she was miserable. Her tears were always just under the surface, ready to spill over at the slightest thought of Roy. But what would happen if she took a chance and went to him? Would he be glad to see her? Or would he order her to never set a foot on his place again?

With a heavy sigh, Justine closed her eyes. ''I don't know what to do anymore, Rose. It doesn't appear that Roy wants me in his life—and maybe that's for the best. My home is here, and I wouldn't want to leave you with the burden of taking care of this ranch by yourself.''

A moment passed in silence before Justine opened her eyes to see Rose shaking her head.

''Justine,'' she said with tender patience, ''if you're worried that marrying Roy would be deserting me, then you have your priorities messed up. You belong with Roy. You and he and Charlie are a family.''

Justine desperately wanted the three of them to be a family. But was there any chance of that happening now? She was afraid to let herself hope that it could.

''You know, Rose, before Roy found out about Charlie being his son, we'd talked about getting married. And I'd planned on telling you that although I was going to live with Roy, I would still help you financially with the ranch.'' She looked down at the floor as tears threatened to fill her eyes. ''Marrying Roy didn't happen, but at least you know I'll always consider the Bar M as my home, too. No matter what happens in the future.''

Rose pressed her palm against Justine's cheek. ''I was never worried about that,'' she said gently.

Justine lifted her head and gave her sister a small but

grateful smile. "Well, I worry about you, Rose. This ranch is too big and has too many cattle for you to care for it all by yourself. You need help."

"I do need help," Rose agreed. "But I don't know where or how I might get it."

"Isn't there a friend or neighbor you might ask to at least help you with some of the bigger jobs? Like the branding and vaccinating?"

Frowning, Rose shook her head. "Most of my friends are schoolteachers. They don't know anything about caring for cattle. And as for a neighbor, well, the closest one we have is Harlan Hamilton, and I certainly wouldn't ask that man to help me do anything," she said with unusual fervor. "There's something about him that…bothers me."

Her brows piqued with sudden curiosity, Justine started to ask Rose just exactly what she had against their neighbor, Harlan Hamilton, but the twins chose that moment to fuss loudly, forcing the two women to fetch them from the playpen.

"I'll get their stroller from the porch," Justine told Rose, "and when I get back from my walk, we'll finish talking about this."

Later, as the evening sun sank below the mountains in the west, Justine pushed the twins down the dirt road toward the river. Charlie happily skipped in a circle around his mother and his new little aunt and uncle.

"Mommy, when will Adam and Anna be able to walk?"

She looked down at the babies, who were always fascinated to be outdoors. The night Roy told her he'd discovered the facts of their birth, she hadn't thought to ask him about the names listed on the birth certificate. Two days later, copies of the birth certificates had arrived in the mail. No letter or note had accompanied the document, but the return address—Lincoln County Sheriff's Department—had told Justine and the rest of the family that Roy had obviously sent it.

Belinda Waller had named Tomas Murdock's babies
Tanya and Timothy. But Justine and her sisters had decided
they knew the babies as Adam and Anna, and they preferred to keep calling the children by the names they had
chosen. If Chloe did get the chance to adopt them, as she
wanted to, their names would be legally changed to stay
that way.

"Oh, it won't be too much longer," she answered Charlie. "Pretty soon they'll be able to stand up all by themselves. And then they'll take a step or two."

"Then will they be able to walk to the barn with me?"

Justine gave her son a wan smile. "No. They'll be too
tottery for that. Next year they'll be able to walk to the
barn with you. And then you can show them Thundercloud
and all of Aunt Chloe's racehorses."

Charlie thought about that for a moment. "But we might
not be here next year, Mommy."

She shot her son a puzzled look. "Why wouldn't we be
here? The Bar M is our home, Charlie."

"I know," he said, then continued his skipping just in
front of the baby carriage. "But we might be living at Sheriff Roy's house next year."

Justine was so shocked, she brought the baby stroller to
a sudden halt. "What makes you say that, son?" she asked
carefully.

Charlie tilted his head, first one way and then the other,
as though he considered his mother's question very ignorant. "Because Sheriff Roy is my daddy. And little boys
like me are supposed to live with their daddies."

With a weary sigh, Justine passed a hand over her forehead. She'd made a vow to herself to stay away from Roy.
He'd ordered her out of his house and out of his life. But
now she knew she was going to have to see him. Their
son's happiness depended on them coming to some sort of
peace. Hopefully, for Charlie's sake, she could make Roy
see that.

Squatting down on her heels, she motioned for Charlie to come to her. "Honey, I know you love Sheriff Roy, and that's good. Little boys are supposed to love their daddies. But he's lived alone for a long time. He might not want us to move into his house."

Smiling with pure confidence, Charlie shook his head. "You don't understand, Mommy. Sheriff Roy loves us. You and me." He touched his finger to his own chest and then to his mother's. "He wants us to live with him. He's just been too busy to come tell us. But he will. I know it!"

Oh, dear God, she prayed as her heart broke into bits and pieces. What was she going to do? How could she protect Charlie from having his heart broken by rejection?

Before she could think of some sort of reply, the sound of an approaching vehicle brought her head up. Over Charlie's head, she could see Roy's Bronco and a trail of dust speeding toward them.

Charlie twisted his head around to look, then let out a loud yip of pleasure. "See, Mommy. I told you he'd come! I told you!"

Justine tried to smile, but it was almost impossible to do when her insides were shaking so badly she could hardly stand. She seriously doubted that Roy had come to make any sort of amends with her. He might have had an urge to see Charlie. But more than likely, she figured, he was coming with news about the twins' mother. Maybe he'd found her! Maybe Belinda Waller was coming back to reclaim the twins!

As soon as he spotted Justine and the children, Roy slacked the Bronco's speed to a crawl. Once he reached them, he pulled to the side of the dirt road and killed the engine.

For the first time in Roy's life, fear rushed through him like a tidal wave, the same sort of fear that he'd seen in the Sanchez woman's eyes when she told him about her missing son.

Up until an hour ago, Roy had been searching the desert hills for Jorge. He'd finally found the little boy and his dog in the bottom of a deep arroyo. Thankfully, the child had been unharmed, and he'd had the pleasure of returning him to his mother.

Ms. Sanchez had been lucky. She hadn't lost her son completely. But had Roy lost his? Had it taken him too long to get past his anger, to realize how much he needed Charlie? And his mother?

Slowly Roy climbed down from the Bronco. Charlie, who'd been clutching a fold of his mother's skirt, ran to him.

"Hi, Sheriff Roy!"

Roy squatted down on his boot heels to be on the boy's level. His heart ached with love as he looked into his son's freckled, beaming face. "Hi, Charlie. How have you been?"

"I've been good." He glanced back at his mother, gave her a big I-told-you-so grin, then turned back to Roy. "I told Mommy you would come. But she didn't believe me."

Roy glanced over Charlie's head to where Justine still stood beside the twins. Her face was unmoving, and he wondered sickly if he'd managed to kill all the love she'd ever felt for him.

"She didn't think I'd come, eh?" Roy asked as he glanced back down at Charlie's happy face.

Charlie shook his head. "Nope. But I knew you would. 'Cause Mommy told me that you're my daddy."

Surprise flicked Roy's eyes up to Justine. She gave him one solemn nod, and his heart soared with inexplicable joy.

"And what do you think about that?"

Charlie reached out and stroked Roy's cheek with the same loving reverence he'd stroked Levi's face. "I'm real glad! I always wanted a daddy, and now I have one that's the sheriff, too!"

Roy couldn't say anything. There was a lump as big as

Texas in his throat. He clutched the child tightly against his chest and held him there for long moments.

"I'm pretty glad about it, too, partner," Roy said huskily.

Charlie squirmed his head back far enough to look up at Roy. "Are me and Mommy gonna live with you now?"

Roy glanced once again at Justine. She was still standing completely still beside the baby stroller. The evening breeze ruffled a gauze skirt around her ankles and fluttered the coral scarf tied in her long hair. She was the most gorgeous, exciting woman he'd ever seen. No matter what happened in the past or what might happen in the future, he would always love her. He knew that as surely as he knew this valley.

"Your mommy and I are going to have a long talk about that," he told Charlie.

Rising to his full height, he walked over to Justine. "Do you want to ride up to the house?"

Justine shook her head, her heart refusing to believe, to hope, that the three of them would ever be a family. Roy was as unpredictable as the desert wind, and she'd had her hopes dashed too many times to put any faith in him now.

"No," she said. "Charlie can ride with you. I'll push the twins back."

Roy looked as if he wanted to argue with her, but he just nodded and loaded Charlie into the Bronco.

After the vehicle had pulled away and eased its way on toward the ranch house, Justine pushed the twins slowly back up the slope of the mountain.

Seeing Roy's tender reaction to their son a moment ago had shaken her. For the past two weeks, she'd firmly convinced herself that he was a heartless, selfish man. But she wasn't the sort of woman who could love a man like that. And she did still love Roy. She'd known that the moment she looked up and saw his Bronco coming toward her.

So what was she going to do now? Marry him so that

Charlie could live with his father and Roy could be with his son? Would knowing Charlie was happy be enough for her?

Back at the house, she turned the sleepy twins over to Chloe, then walked out to the courtyard, where Roy was kneeling beside Charlie on his sandpile.

When Roy saw Justine approaching them, he rose and went to meet her. For the first time since he'd arrived, she noticed he was dressed as though he'd just gotten off the job. His gun was still strapped to his hips, his badge still pinned to his khaki shirt. She couldn't help but be struck by his tough masculinity, and yet there was a weariness about his face that made him vulnerable somehow.

"Don't let me take you away from Charlie," she told him. "He's been dying to see you for a long time."

His blue eyes lovingly touched her face. He couldn't imagine what it must have been like for her to carry his baby alone, to give birth to and raise him alone and away from her family. And she'd done it all out of love, he realized. Love for him and for their baby.

"I wished I'd come sooner."

Her heart felt as if a hand were squeezing it. She drew in a long breath in hopes of easing the pain.

"I wish you had, too. For Charlie's sake."

"I'm not here solely for Charlie's sake," he said.

Her brows lifted. "For your own?"

Roy took her by the arm, led her past Charlie and out the back entrance of the courtyard.

"Charlie won't—" she began, only to have him interrupt her.

"I've already explained to our son that his mother and daddy are going to have a long talk by themselves. He understands."

"Apparently more than I do," she said with a weary sigh. "He believes you love him."

"I do. More than you'll ever know."

"He believes you love me, too."

"He's right. I do."

Unable to hide the pain in her eyes, she glanced at him sharply. "You don't have to tell me that, Roy. I'm not going to try to stop you from seeing Charlie. You're his father. I want you to *be* his father."

He guided her over to a stand of pine trees. The shade was deep and cool, and the breeze sang through the boughs above their heads. Justine leaned her back against the largest trunk.

"I'm not saying anything I don't mean, Justine. You and I—we've gone too far to be skipping around the truth now."

She slowly searched his eyes, and what she found there made her heart melt like chocolate candy in the warm sun.

"I don't understand you, Roy. You ordered me out of your house."

He grimaced. "I was angry and hurt. I couldn't believe that I'd been cheated out of five years of my child's life."

Tears filled her eyes. "That wasn't the way I wanted it to be, Roy. Not for you or me, or Charlie."

He took her hand and clasped it tightly between the two of his. "I know that. It was just hard to accept that you kept his existence from me for so long."

Justine shook her head with deep regret. It was as Rose had said, she thought. Both of them had done what they believed was right, yet all of them had wound up being hurt.

"To be honest, Roy, I came back to the Hondo Valley with intentions of never seeing you again, or telling you about Charlie. Our affair had been over for a long time. You'd married Marla, and I certainly didn't think you'd want anything to do with me. Or a ready-made family."

With a groan, he tugged her head against his shoulder and held her tightly against him. "You can't imagine how many times down through the years I'd wished it had been you who'd come to me and told me you were pregnant with my child. Then, to find out that you really had been... It crushes me, Justine. To think of all the wasted time you and I and Charlie could have had together. Instead, we were kept apart, because of Marla's lies.''

She lifted her head to look at him. "It's been two weeks since you found out about Charlie. I thought you'd decided to put us out of your life."

"It's not easy for me to forgive or forget, Justine," he admitted with a rueful twist to his face. "For the first few days, I was so angry I couldn't see straight. Then I began to miss you both terribly, and I knew that if I was ever going to be happy I was going to have to do what you said and put the past behind me. I have, Justine." His hands reached up and gently framed her face. "I've spent the bigger part of today searching for a missing boy not much older than Charlie. His parents are separated, and he thought he could walk all the way to Alto to see his father."

Justine gasped with fear for the unknown child. "Did you find him?"

Roy nodded. "He was crying and scared, but safe."

"Thank God."

"Yes, thank God. I tell you, Justine, when I found that boy, I vowed to myself that Charlie would never have to be without his father. And that you would never have to experience the terror his mother went through before we returned her son to her."

"Oh, Roy, your job is—" She paused, then swallowed, in an effort to collect her surging emotions. "You do such good things for people, and I'm so very proud of you. But it scares me at times. Especially when I know you're out there tracking down deranged people with guns."

He smiled with gentle understanding. "Justine, I've been a law officer for many years now. I'm well trained. I know how to handle myself in dangerous situations. I promise you, I'll never try to be the hero, or take an unnecessary chance and put myself in the line of fire. Especially now that I have you and Charlie in my life. I want to stay safe and sound for the both of you.''

Suddenly she was sobbing tears of joy. ''You really do mean all of that—don't you?''

Still smiling, he wiped her eyes. ''Of course I mean it. I want to marry you. To give you and Charlie my name.''

She gripped his arms and pressed her cheek against his heart. ''I love you, Roy. I'm going to spend the rest of my life making everything up to you.''

''No,'' he said as he eased her face up to his. ''We both made mistakes. We'll make it up to each other.''

Lowering his head, he kissed her with love and promise and hope. ''Maybe we can have other children, Justine? And this time I can be there to help you. To experience it all with you.''

Her head was reeling with happiness. ''Would you like that?''

He gave her a slow, sexy grin. ''I can't wait to get started,'' he whispered.

Laughing breathlessly, she grabbed his hand and started leading him back toward the house. ''Then we'd better go tell Charlie and the rest of the family.''

''Do you think they'll be happy for us?''

''They'll be thrilled we're getting married,'' she assured him. ''Now, if you could track down the twins' mother and Rose could find someone to help her with the cattle, everything would be so much better for all of us.''

''I promise I'll help your family as much as I can, Justine. The future is going to get better. Starting now. With the two of us,'' he whispered, his blue eyes sparkling with love.

''Well, I'm sure Aunt Kitty is going to insist on toasting the good news.'' Her eyes suddenly widened with mischief, and she began to laugh. ''Speaking of drinking a toast,

Rose just bought a new jug of apple cider. I'm sure she'd open it for you.''

Laughing, he caught her by the waist and tugged her into the circle of his arms. ''I think it's time I paid you back for that little shower you gave me.''

''Roy!''

Her squeal was blotted out by his kiss, and as the last rays of light fell behind the mountains in the distance, Justine took sweet punishment from the sheriff of Lincoln County.

* * * * *

twins
on the doorstep
by Stella Bagwell

When the Murdock sisters found abandoned twins
on their ranch-house doorstep, they had no clue the
little ones would lead them to love!

Come see how each sister meets her match—and how
the twins' family is discovered—in

THE SHERIFF'S SON (SR #1218, April 1997)

THE RANCHER'S BRIDE (SR #1224, May 1997)

THE TYCOON'S TOTS (SR #1228, June 1997)

TWINS ON THE DOORSTEP—a brand-new miniseries
by Stella Bagwell starting in April...
Only from

Silhouette ROMANCE™

In April 1997
Bestselling Author

takes her Family Circle series to new heights with

In April 1997 Dallas Schulze brings readers a
brand-new, longer, out-of-series title featuring the
characters from her popular Family Circle miniseries.

When rancher Keefe Walker found Tessa Wyndham he
knew that she needed a man's protection—she was
pregnant, alone and on the run from a heartless past.
Keefe was also hiding from a dark past...but in one
overwhelming moment he and Tessa forged a family
bond that could never be broken.

Available in April wherever books are sold.

Silhouette Romance proudly invites you
to get to know the members of

The Single
Daddy Club

a new miniseries by award-winning author
Donna Clayton

Derrick: Ex-millitary man who unexpectedly
falls into fatherhood
MISS MAXWELL BECOMES A MOM (March '97)

Jason: Widowed daddy desperately in need of some live-in help
NANNY IN THE NICK OF TIME (April '97)

Reece: Single and satisfied father of one about
to meet his Ms. Right
BEAUTY AND THE BACHELOR DAD (May '97)

Don't miss any of these heartwarming stories as
three single dads say bye-bye to their bachelor days.
Only from

▼ *Silhouette* ROMANCE™
TM

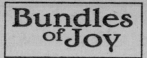

Bundles of Joy

The biggest romantic surprises come in the smallest packages!

January:

HAVING GABRIEL'S BABY by Kristin Morgan (#1199)
After one night of passion Joelle was expecting! The dad-to-be, rancher Gabriel Lafleur, insisted on marriage. But could they find true love as a family?

April:

YOUR BABY OR MINE? by Marie Ferrarella (#1216)
Single daddy Alec Beckett needed help with his infant daughter! When the lovely Marissa Rogers took the job with an infant of her own, Alec realized he wanted this mom-for-hire *permanently*—as part of a real family!

Don't miss these irresistible Bundles of Joy,
coming to you in January and April,
only from

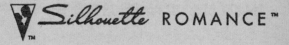